THE
MYSTIFIED MAGISTRATE
AND OTHER TALES

OTHER WORKS BY THE MARQUIS DE SADE
TRANSLATED BY RICHARD SEAVER

Justine, Philosophy in the Bedroom, & Other Writings
(with Austryn Wainhouse)

The 120 Days of Sodom & Other Writings
(with Austryn Wainhouse)

Letters from Prison

THE
MYSTIFIED MAGISTRATE
AND OTHER TALES

MARQUIS DE SADE

Translated and with an Introduction
by Richard Seaver

ARCADE PUBLISHING • NEW YORK

FIRST ENGLISH-LANGUAGE EDITION

Library of Congress Cataloging-in-Publication Data
Sade, marquis de, 1740–1814
    [Short stories. English. Selections]
    The mystified magistrate and other tales / Marquis de Sade; translated and with an introduction by Richard Seaver.
        p. cm.
    ISBN 1-55970-432-2 (hc)
    ISBN 1-55970-579-5 (pb)
    1. Sade, marquis de, 1740–1814—Translations into English.
I. Seaver, Richard. II. Title.
PQ2063.S3 A275 2000
843'.6—dc21   00-23110

Published in the United States by Arcade Publishing, Inc., New York
Distributed by Time Warner Trade Publishing

Visit our Web site at www.arcadepub.com

10 9 8 7 6 5 4 3 2 1

Designed by API

FG

PRINTED IN THE UNITED STATES OF AMERICA

CONTENTS

INTRODUCTION

Sade's novella "The Mystified Magistrate" was written while the author was a prisoner in the Bastille and was completed, as he meticulously notes at the end of the manuscript, "at ten o'clock in the evening on July 16, 1787"—thus almost two years to the day before that bastion was stormed at the outbreak of the French Revolution.

The story is contemporary with Sade's slightly longer novella, *"Les Infortunes de la vertu"* (The Misfortunes of Virtue), which he finished only a week earlier, on July 8, 1787, after two weeks of intensive writing. One hundred thirty-eight pages in its original form, "The Misfortunes of Virtue" was reworked and expanded by Sade during the following year and was eventually published in 1791—a year after his liberation from the Charenton Insane Asylum—as the full-length novel *Justine*, considered by many to be his masterpiece. Six years later, having miraculously escaped the merciful blade of Dr. Guillotine, Sade further expanded the story into the monstrous *La Nouvelle Justine*, an even more daring and outrageous version of the virtuous heroine's travails.

The composition of "The Mystified Magistrate," therefore, and the rest of these tales, dates from one of Sade's most fruitful and creative periods. The marquis was then in his forties, and in spite of growing obesity[1] and problems with his eyesight (in the margin of the last manuscript page of "The Misfortunes of Virtue," Sade wrote: "All the time I was writing this my eyes were bothering me"), his mind was vigorous and active and he was obsessively clear about what his life work was to be. Two years before penning "The Mystified Magistrate" and the other stories in this collection, Sade had written, also in the Bastille, his most seminal work, *The 120 Days of Sodom*, which the French critic Maurice Heine, who in the early decades of the twentieth century almost single-handedly resurrected Sade from near oblivion, has called "the first positive effort to classify sexual anomalies . . . a century before Krafft-Ebing and Freud."

Although Sade has never been especially reputed as a humorist, there are throughout his work flashes of mordant wit, irony, and a keen sense of the grotesque: one need only recall *Justine*'s description of the avaricious couple, Monsieur and Madame Harpin, or any number of comically absurd situations in *Philosophy in the Bedroom*. "The Mystified Magistrate" and some of the stories here, however, are perhaps Sade's only works in which humor is dominant and pervasive. In writing them, Sade took Boccaccio as his model, or rather, mentor.

The principal character of the novella, and object of Sade's impassioned ridicule, Judge Fontanis, is patterned after one or more of the judges of the High Court of Aix. It was this same court that fifteen years earlier, on September 11, 1772, had sentenced the author and his footman Latour to death. The crime of which they stood accused—and it was a capital crime—was the poisoning of and perpetration of unnatural acts (read "sodomy") upon a group of Marseilles prostitutes Sade had engaged during his visit to that city in the summer of that same year. The "poisoning" was the result of Sade's having given two, and perhaps three, of the girls some aniseed candy, the sugar of which had been soaked with Spanish fly extract, or cantharides. It is clear that Sade's intention during that *partouze* morning of June 27, 1772, was not to poison but to excite. But in all probability the candies in question were homemade, and either they contained more cantharides than was intended or Sade in his own excitement urged more upon the girls than their systems could endure.

As for the accusation of sodomy—also a capital offense—all four girls subsequently denied to the royal prosecutor that they had participated in any such act, citing God as their witness. The gentleman in question had indeed asked them to perform such an act, they admitted, but, decent girls that they were, they had steadfastly refused. Based on their collective withdrawal of that allegation, and the subsequent, more thorough analysis of the cantharides, which revealed no evidence of any poison "either bichloride of mercury or arsenic," the case against Sade should have collapsed. But there was hanky-panky not only on the back benches but also— and especially—on the front,[2] and as a result the royal prosecutor's case was upheld and Sade, from that day forward, became not only a fugitive from justice but a marked man, a symbol of the hated aristocratic privilege, of the unjust society of haves and have-nots spawned by the egomaniacal excesses of Louis XIV, nurtured and brought to a new (degenerative) level by Louis XV, and carried to its bloody conclusion under Louis XVI.

After lengthy depositions, medical reports, and the aforementioned pharmaceutical analyses, the royal prosecutor found, and the High Court of Aix confirmed, that the crimes of the marquis and his domestic Latour were to be expiated at the cathedral door and that they were thereafter to be taken to the Place Saint-Louis, "for, on a gallows, the said Sade to be decapitated . . . and the said Latour to be hanged by the neck and strangled; then the body of the said Sade and that of the said Latour to be burned and their ashes strewn to the wind." Since both Sade and his footman had fled to Italy roughly a week after the "Marseilles Affair," the sentence was, fortunately for them and for history, carried out only in effigy. But this notorious scandal, which was seized upon and made into banner headlines by the popular press of the day, had serious repercussions throughout France and was a major factor in creating the legend that surrounded Sade both during his lifetime and ever since.

One of the judges of the Aix high court was a certain Monsieur de Fontiene, whose name bears a remarkable resemblance to that of the protagonist of "The Mystified Magistrate." Whether it was actually he or another of the judges—or, more likely, a composite of the entire thirteen-member panel—whom Sade was holding up to ridicule remains a matter of conjecture. There is no question, however, that the unduly harsh sentence of 1772 prompted Sade to take his literary revenge: there are several references in "The Mystified Magistrate" and in the other stories here not only to the judges' collusive protection of whores in Provence but also to the unjust, harsh, and stupid sentence the High Court of Aix had once imposed on a worthy young nobleman of the region. "It was I who last year talked my learned colleagues into exiling from the province for a period of ten years—and thereby ruining forever—a nobleman who had already served his king faithfully and well,"[3] confesses Judge Fontanis one evening when he has imbibed a bit too much wine. "And all that over a party of females."

Later in "The Mystified Magistrate," the Marquis d'Olincourt—a spokesman for and alter ego of Sade—comments acidly on the colic from which Judge Fontanis is suffering. "You'll have to excuse him if he took this attack a trifle seriously," says d'Olincourt. "It is an illness of some consequence in Marseilles or Aix, this minor movement of the bowels. Ever since we have seen a troop of rogues—colleagues of our friend here present—judge that a few whores who were suffering from colic were 'poisoned,' it should come as no surprise to us that colic is a serious matter indeed as far as a judge from Provence is concerned."[4]

Sade's scathing condemnation of the judiciary is also evidenced in his hilarious put-down "The Windbags of Provence," in which he combines judicial ignorance and arrogance into a visually devastating farce. But if he views the judiciary with utter disdain, he also, in "Emilie de Tourville," castigates those who take justice into their own hands. Although he changes the setting, the sex, and the situation, Sade is clearly comparing this case of gross injustice on the part of Emilie's jealous brothers to his own desperate situation. By the time he penned these lively tales, Sade had already spent more than ten years behind bars for his presumed crimes, and especially as a result of the Aix sentence in absentia. His mother-in-law, the Présidente de Montreuil,[5] upset by her son-in-law's infidelities and increasingly public and politicized acts of sexual rebellion, set about petitioning the king and paying off justices to get—and keep—her son-in-law incarcerated. As in the story "Emilie de Tourville," Sade's letters are filled with recriminations against those who, taking matters into their own hands, do far more damage than any judicial system, however stupid and corrupt.

Other stories in this collection deal with themes near and dear to Sade, all of which reflect the tenor of his time. Hypocrisy was rampant in the land: in the eighteenth century, that husbands betrayed wives was not news, but to have wives of the aristocracy and upper bourgeoisie consciously and brazenly betraying their husbands was ("The Properly Punished Pimp"; "An Eye for an Eye"; "Room for Two"). In "The Husband Who Turned Priest," that same theme is echoed and overlaid with a topping of the debauchery and degradation of the Church. Other tales deal openly with homosexuality and lesbianism. In "Augustine de Villebranche" Sade-the-philosopher states, well ahead of his time, that if Nature indeed has inclined a person to favor those of his or her own sex, it would be wrong for society to condemn them for what were thought of as "unnatural crimes."

Whatever their merit, Sade viewed these stories as a light counterpoint to his dark, consciously clandestine works—*La Nouvelle Justine, Juliette,* and *The 120 Days of Sodom.* Written over several years, first in the dreary prison of Vincennes on the eastern outskirts of Paris where he spent seven hellish years, then in the Bastille, these stories were originally planned as part of a volume to be called *Tales and Little Fables of the XVIIIth Century by a Provençal Troubadour.* In Sade's own words: "These short stories and anecdotes are, in some instances, light-hearted, and even a trifle bawdy, but always well within the boundaries of modesty and decency, while others are serious and tragic."

The volume from which they are drawn was first published in 1926 by Maurice Heine, who meticulously followed Sade's text insofar as it was possible to do so, since large segments of the manuscript—which Sade had projected as a four-volume set, each with its own frontispiece—were lost when the Bastille was stormed and sacked on July 14, 1789. This occurred just ten days after Sade, whom the prison authorities rightly viewed as a troublemaker in that increasingly tense time,[6] had been, in his own words, "torn from his bed naked as a worm" and in the wee hours of July 4 driven through the darkened streets of Paris to the Charenton Insane Asylum, where he remained for another year. After his liberation from Charenton, on Good Friday, 1790 ("I have decided to celebrate it as a holiday for the rest of my life"), Sade almost immediately repaired to the site of his former prison and spent hours poking around in the ruins in search of his precious manuscripts, over whose loss, he wrote to his lawyer Gaufridy, "I am shedding tears of blood." The image of the now corpulent, middle-aged marquis—he was then fifty—clothed not in his aristocratic finery but dressed down in drab Revolutionary-acceptable garb, poking in the charred ashes among the debris of the Bastille is as poignant as it is pathetic.

These stories, Maurice Heine observed, were "very much in keeping with the tenor of their time, a mixture of literature and philosophy, cast in the form of fiction. . . ." He notes further that the final corrected texts had been contained in Sade's *beau cahier* (handsome notebook), which was stripped of its contents except for xiv ✤ THE MARQUIS DE SADE

a few scattered pages; thus the text of his 1926 edition was necessarily based on the *cahier jaune*—the "Yellow Notebook." Therefore, notes Heine, "this publication is based not on the definitive version but on an earlier draft, albeit one that was read and corrected by the author. This basic reservation is important to make, for it explains any oversights or even the extremely rare inaccuracies in the text to which purists might take exception. May they blame any such inconsistencies not on the Marquis de Sade himself—a writer far superior to most of his contemporaries and the first French novelist of the Revolutionary period—but rather on those who have persecuted him and on the irreparable consequences of their efforts to suppress or destroy his works."[7]

To understand—both philosophically and as fiction—not only these stories but indeed all of Sade's voluminous work, one must remember the society out of which they sprang. Born during the reign of Louis XV, Sade grew up in a country steeped in depravity, hypocrisy, and injustice, both during the Regency and the full reign of Louis XV—doubtless the most corrupt and decadent monarch ever to rule France. The four decades prior to July 1789 were marked by the mad, unfettered pursuit of sexual and sensual pleasure by the king and his entourage. The number of the king's mistresses was astounding but, not content with plucking ladies of the court for his dalliances, he had a personal bordello constructed in Versailles in 1750, Le Parc-aux-Cerfs—the Deer Park—to which a nightly supply of young women were brought, at the insistence and under the supervision of his former mistress, Madame de Pompadour. The network of those charged with supplying the king's apparently insatiable appetite spread from one end of the country to the other, directed by an official cabinet minister, La Ferte, whose august title was Intendant de Menus-Plaisirs—Minister of Dainty Pleasures. It has been estimated that, given all the payoffs due various members of this far-flung pleasure syndicate, each girl brought to the Deer Park cost the public treasury as much as a million *livres*. Over the more than two decades of the Deer Park's existence—Louis XV died in 1774—the cost to France was staggering and explains in good part why his successor inherited a country close to financial ruin. The Goncourt brothers, looking for a simple word to best define the eighteenth century, settled on *debauchery*. "Debauchery is the air on which [this century] breathes and lives," they wrote. In *Justine*, Sade himself terms his own era as "the age of total corruption." And in *Juliette*, he bases his character Saint Fond, whose cynicism and egoism matches his corruption, on one of Louis XV's ministers.

If Sade's opus, then, is a ferocious and unrelenting attack on the existing social order, it is also in many ways a mirror of his time—a distorted mirror to be sure, but nonetheless cruelly accurate.

If the royal court and aristocracy were the main dissolute culprits ("When a royal prince walks the way of vice," wrote Sade, "he is accompanied by the entire society"), the French clergy of the eighteenth century also share a fair measure of responsibility. The clergy was in large part made up of members of the aristocracy: oldest sons of the nobility joined the army, younger ones joined the priesthood. In this century of corruption in France, all levels of clergy—bishops, priests, *abbés*—thought

xvi ✦ THE MARQUIS DE SADE

little or nothing of having mistresses or visiting with
almost unrestrained frequency the bordellos that criss-
crossed the land.[8] Louis XV had his vice squads, which
spied and reported upon his subjects' sexual practices
in detail (more for their titillation factor, no doubt, than
their curbing influence) and police records of the time
are filled with accounts of men of the cloth spending virtually as much time in the arms of prostitutes as in the
arms of the Church. Sade's paternal uncle, the Abbé de
Sade, with whom the future author spent five important
and formative years, from the age of five to ten, at the
abbé's Château de Saumane in southern France, had nu-
merous mistresses and was once arrested in a famous
Paris bordello and spent several days in jail. Thus if in
his fiction and philosophical works Sade mercilessly
takes men of the cloth to task for their vices, duplicity, and shameless hypocrisy—as he does here in "The
Teacher Philosopher" and "The Husband Who Turned
Priest"—there is ample pragmatic reason to explain and
justify his position.

Among the many stigmata with which Sade has been
branded is that of being not only anticlerical but an atheist, and indeed he was. But again one must relate his
stance to the times in which he lived: in the eighteenth
century it was, as Maurice Heine observes, "not terribly
original to be an atheist. Since the beginning of the century, there were many of the more daring minds who
considered religion as a pure figment of men's imagina-
tions, metaphysical truths as an illusion, and belief in
God as 'the strongest and most deeply-rooted of preju-

dices.'" Many intellectual groups of the day—philosophers, mathematicians, doctors—made it mandatory for
new members to proclaim their atheism before being admitted. In 1750—the same year Louis XV built his Deer
Park—works by La Mettrie, Diderot, and Baron d'Hol-
bach "dared bring [atheism] out from the clandestinity to
which it had hitherto been relegated for so long," Heine
notes.

Thus Sade, the ultimate rebel, was in a sense simply
espousing a movement that, while still a countercurrent,
was fast becoming mainstream. Sade's problem was, as
usual, his total lack of discretion. While others kept their
atheism closeted, or resorted to publishing their works
abroad, Sade made no bones about his position, as if provoking the authorities to react. One of his first brushes
with the law, in fact, was the result of his having taken
what with anyone else would have been an evening's
dalliance with a prostitute. Instead it became a national
scandal. To be precise: on the night of October 18,
1763—Sade was then twenty-three—he took a woman
named Jeanne Testard to his rented room on the rue
Mouffetard near the Sorbonne and there, instead of simply enjoying himself, spent the night blaspheming God,
Christ, and the Virgin Mary, obliging Jeanne to do the
same. As might be expected, the next morning Jeanne—
God-fearing girl that she was—complained of her ordeal
to her procuress, who in turn complained to the police.
In less than two weeks, Sade was arrested and imprisoned for the first time in that dismal dungeon Vincennes,
where he later would spend so many agonizing years.
The charge was blasphemy and profanation, far more

serious crimes in the eyes of Louis XV's laws than that of simple debauchery.

Sade spent twenty-seven years—half his adult life— in eleven prisons under five different regimes, doubtless a record, most certainly for someone whose major crime was committing "the English vice" with paid prostitutes. Sade was not jailed for crimes against the state nor society. As a self-proclaimed, and certainly unrepentant, libertine, he was no more guilty of heinous crimes than were hundreds if not thousands of his contemporaries, none of whom suffered penalties remotely resembling those meted out to Sade. Rather, his "crime" was flaunting his "misdeeds," as he refers to his sexual escapades, of openly proclaiming his preferences and predilections. In so doing he offended the king, whose pompous court he assiduously eschewed; the clergy, whose hypocrisy he abhorred; and his family-in-law, whose recent escutcheon[9] he badly stained. But if the king was ultimately forgiving and the clergy generally indifferent, his mother-in-law, Madame la Présidente de Montreuil, was bound and determined to see her son-in-law removed from society. It is through her—doubtless with the tacit if not active approval of her husband, a well-meaning, weak-willed man—that Sade spent the thirteen years between 1777 and 1790 in dungeons. And it was she who, unknowingly but unequivocally, by removing her son-in-law from society, was responsible for turning him into a writer. The longer this "freest spirit that ever lived" (Apollinaire) remained locked up, the more wild the demons that filled his brain were set loose to people a fictional universe such as the world had never seen, to propound a philosophy that—until precisely two hundred years after his birth in 1740—few could comprehend or even imagine, a world in which cold, calculated evil triumphed at every turn.

It is all too easy to condemn Sade, as many have done, as mad, and thus dismiss his works as aberrations, pure and simple, best left unread, perhaps even burned.[10] That the "monster author" (Napoleon Bonaparte) was an inveterate libertine, that he was openly bisexual, as much enamored of feminine beauty as he was of the callipygian portion of the human body, is uncontested. That the years behind bars affected his health as well as whetted his imagination to unbelievable heights (and depths) none would dispute. But as we have seen, Sade was less an incomprehensible aberration than a product of his age, one who, admittedly, seized the various strands of the social fabric and rearranged them into a diabolic anarchical pattern, standing the world, as it were, upside down. Much of his philosophical work, and indeed his personal letters that have survived, reveal a man who was as intelligent as he was intolerant, as principled as he was violent, as sensitive as he was arrogant. But he was certainly not mad.

Perhaps understandably, the stories in this volume, which reveal the lighter, sometimes comic side of the Marquis de Sade, were among the first of many volumes discovered—or rediscovered—in the twentieth century that give us a fuller, more rounded picture of this amazing—and amazingly complicated—man. Unlike some of the other works, these tales should offend no one. Rather, it is hoped that they might, as the author noted, give the reader a modicum of pleasure, and perhaps an insight or two.

In the stories, the footnotes at the bottoms of the pages are Sade's own. The notes at the back of the book are the translator's.

A NOTE ABOUT MONEY

In these stories, Sade mentions various monies current in the eighteenth century: *écus*, *louis*, *livres*, *francs*, *pistoles*, and *sous*. The *écu*, a silver coin first struck under the reign of Louis IX, or Saint Louis (1214–1270), was worth three *livres*, the *louis* twenty-four *livres*. The value of the *livre* varied considerably, depending on the historical moment, and was replaced by the franc. The *livre* and franc seem to have been of relatively equal value; before 1789 the term franc was used loosely to mean *livre*. The *pistole*, an ancient gold coin also of varying value from country to country, was worth ten francs in France. The *sou* was worth five centimes, or 1/20th of a franc.

To give an idea of the cost of living in 1789, a semi-skilled worker made 25 or 30 *sous* a day; a skilled laborer as much as 50 *sous*. A provincial bourgeois could live comfortably on 3,000 *livres* a year. In a letter to his wife Sade writes despairingly that it had cost the family a hundred thousand francs to have him incarcerated for ten years, or ten thousand francs per annum for room and board at Vincennes and the Bastille. For her own room and board at the convent of Saint-Aure, Madame de Sade paid half that amount for quarters she described as far from luxurious. Monsieur de Rougemont, warden of Vincennes prison, earned a salary of 18,000 francs a year (which he augmented, according to Sade and other prisoners, by an additional "illegal" 15,000 francs annually, overcharging his wards for food, wine, and other necessities).

The
Mystified Magistrate

And Other Tales

THE MYSTIFIED MAGISTRATE

> Ah! trust in me, I wish to sing their praises
> In such wise ... that for twenty years
> they'll dare not show their faces.

*I*t was with the most profound regret that the Marquis d'Olincourt, a colonel of dragoons, a man of wit, grace, and vivacity, saw his sister-in-law, Mademoiselle de Téroze, promised in marriage to one of the most dreadful creatures who has ever existed upon the face of the earth. This charming girl, eighteen years of age, as fresh as the mythical Flora, fashioned like the Graces themselves, had for four years been the object of the affections of young Count d'Elbène—he being the lieutenant-colonel of d'Olincourt's regiment. With great trepidation she saw that fatal moment arrive which, by joining her to the grumpy spouse to whom she had been betrothed, would separate her forever from the only man who was truly worthy of her. But how could she avoid it? Mademoiselle de Téroze's father was a stubborn old fellow, a hypochondriac who was plagued with the gout, a man who sadly fancied that it was neither propriety nor a person's virtues that ought to govern a girl's feelings about a husband but only reason, maturity, and above all position. He further fancied that the position of a man of the long robe—a judge—was the most esteemed, the most majestic of all positions under the monarchy—the one, moreover, he loved most in all the world. It therefore followed, as night follows day, that only with a man of the judiciary could his daughter be happy.

In spite of these sentiments, old Baron de Téroze had nevertheless given his elder daughter in marriage to a military man who, more's the pity, was a colonel of dragoons. This daughter, extremely happy and born for happiness in many respects, had no reason to regret her father's choice. But all this in no wise altered her father's opinion; if this first marriage had been a success, it was merely the exception that proved the rule; the fact remained that only a man of the robe could make a girl completely happy. With this premise clearly established, it had then become a question of finding a judge. Now, of all the possible judges, the most amiable in the eyes of the old baron was a certain Monsieur de Fontanis, presiding judge of the High Court of Aix, an old Provençal acquaintance. Therefore, without further ado, it was Monsieur de Fontanis who was chosen to become Mademoiselle de Téroze's husband.

Few people have a clear picture of a presiding judge of the Court of Aix, for it is a species of animal of whom much has been said and little understood, a strict moralist by profession, meticulous, credulous, stubborn, vain, a timid soul, talkative and stupid by nature; his face stretched and taut like a gosling, rolling his *r*'s like Punch, and generally tall, thin, gaunt, and as smelly as an old corpse . . . It was as though all the spleen and inflexibility of the kingdom's magistrature had taken refuge in the Provençal temple of Themis[1] in order to sally forth from there each time a French court wanted to admonish someone or hang one of its citizens. But Monsieur de Fontanis surpassed by at least a full degree this rough sketch of his compatriots. Above his frail frame, which was slightly stooped, one could note that the back of his low-set head sloped upward toward the top; his brow was a sallow, almost sickly yellow and the pate itself was adorned magisterially by a multipurpose wig, the likes of which had yet to be seen in Paris. His two slightly bowed legs supported, with relative pomp and circumstance, this walking clock tower from whose upper respiratory tract there issued forth, not without more than a few drawbacks for anyone who happened to be in the vicinity, a shrill voice emphatically uttering idle banter, half in French and half in Provençal, banter he never failed to laugh at with his mouth open so wide that one could, at these moments, see a blackish abyss clear down to the uvula, a toothless pit excoriated in certain places and that bore an undeniable resemblance to another bodily seat which, considering the makeup of our frail humanity, as frequently becomes the throne of kings as it does of peasants. Quite apart from these physical attractions, Monsieur de Fontanis laid claim to a fine mind: after having dreamt one night that he had ascended to the third heaven with Saint Paul, he considered himself the greatest astronomer in all France. He took legal stands like Farinacci and Cujas,[2] and he was often heard to say, in keeping with these great men, and with his colleagues who were not great men, that a citizen's life, his fortune, honor, and family—in short, everything that society holds sacred—are as nothing when it comes to ferreting out crime, and that it was a hundred times better to risk the lives of a dozen innocent souls than to let a single guilty person go free by mistake, because there is justice in heaven above even though it be lacking in the courts here below, and because the punishment of an innocent soul has no other drawback than to send a soul on his way to paradise, whereas to let a guilty person go free threatens to multiply crime on earth. The only kind of people who had any influence on Monsieur de Fontanis's hardened soul were whores—not that he generally used them to any great extent himself. Although of a very ardent temper, he was stubborn by nature and inclined to use his forces sparingly, so that his desires always far exceeded his ability to fulfill them. Monsieur de Fontanis aspired to the glory of transmitting his illustrious name to posterity, it was as simple as that, but what led this famous judge to be indulgent with the priestesses of Venus was his conviction that there were few citizens, at least on the distaff side, who were more useful to the State. Through their double-dealing, he claimed, their lies, and their loose tongues, a whole host of secret crimes managed to be uncovered. You had to give Monsieur de Fontanis due credit at least on one score, and that was that he was the sworn enemy of what philosophers are wont to call human frailties.

This slightly grotesque combination of a physical Ostrogoth and Justinian morality left the town of Aix for the first time in his life in April, 1779, at the behest of the Baron de Téroze—whom he had known for a long time, for reasons of little or no interest to the reader—and came to take up lodgings at the Hotel de Danemark, not far from the Baron's residence. Since it was then the time of year when the Saint-Germain fair was being held, everyone in the hotel thought that this extraordinary-looking creature had come to town as part of the show. One of those semi-official characters who are forever offering their services in public places such as these even went so far as to propose that he go inform the impresario Nicolet, who would be more than delighted to fit him into the program, unless of course he would prefer to make his debut with the rival impresario Audinot. To which the judge replied:*

"My nurse was careful to warn me when I was a child that the Parisians are a caustic bunch much given to practical jokes, and would never properly appreciate my many virtues. But my wig-maker was quick to add, nonetheless, that my wig would make a deep impression on them. The common people are wont to joke when they are dying of hunger, to sing when they are overwhelmed with burdens! . . . Oh, I have always maintained that what these people need is an Inquisition like the one in Madrid, or a scaffold constantly ready and waiting, like the one in Aix."

And yet Monsieur de Fontanis, after freshening up a bit—which could only have had the effect of heightening the splendor of his sexagenarian charms—and after spraying himself with some rose-water and lavender which, as Horace says, were in no wise ambitious adornments, after all this, I say, and perhaps a few other precautions that have not been brought to our attention, the judge came to pay a call upon his old friend the baron.

---

*The reader is reminded that he must try to supply Monsieur de Fontanis's Provençal accent, to imagine him rolling his *r*'s, qualities the written word simply cannot convey.

The double doors swing open, his name is announced, and the judge enters.

Unfortunately for him, the two sisters and the Marquis d'Olincourt[3] were playing like three children in one corner of the salon when this highly original figure of a man appeared, and no matter how hard they tried to control themselves they could not refrain from bursting out laughing, with the result that the Provençal judge's solemn face was thoroughly discountenanced. He had been at great pains to study, in front of a mirror, the bow he planned to make upon his arrival, and he was performing it reasonably well when that accursed peal of laughter from the lips of our three young friends caused him to remain bent over, in the form of an arc, a great deal longer than he had planned to. He finally did straighten up, however; a stern glance from the baron brought his three children back within the bounds of respect, and the conversation began.

The baron, whose mind was already made up and who did not want to waste any time beating around the bush, informed Mademoiselle de Téroze, before this initial meeting had come to an end, that the judge was the man he had in mind for her to marry and that before the week was out he expected her to give him her hand. Mademoiselle de Téroze said nothing, the judge withdrew, and the baron said once again that he expected to be obeyed.

It was a cruel situation the lovely girl found herself in: not only did she adore Monsieur d'Elbène, not only did he idolize her, but, what is more, she was as weak as she was soft-hearted, and unfortunately had allowed her charming lover to pluck that flower which, so different from the rose to which it is nonetheless sometimes compared, does not have the rose's ability to be reborn each spring. That being the case, what would Monsieur de Fontanis... a presiding judge of the court of Aix... have thought upon perceiving that his task had already been accomplished? A Provençal magistrate may have his share of ridiculous qualities—they are indeed inherent in this class—but the fact remains that he is well versed in the matter of first fruits, and can understandably be expected to find them at least once in his life, in his wife. This was what gave Mademoiselle de Téroze pause, for, however quick-witted and mischievous by nature, she was nonetheless of a sensitivity quite befitting a woman in such a situation and understood perfectly well that her husband would indeed have a very low opinion of her if she were to provide him with proof that she had been disrespectful to him even before she had had the honor of meeting him. For nothing is so just as our prejudices on this matter: not only must a poor wretch of a girl sacrifice all the affections of which her heart is capable to the husband her parents choose for her, but she is even guilty if, before meeting the tyrant who has been chosen to enslave her, she has had the misfortune to listen to the voice of Nature and yield, be it only for a moment, to its promptings.

Mademoiselle de Téroze therefore confided her concerns to her sister, who, more playful than she was prudish, more pleasure-prone than religious, reacted to the secret by bursting out laughing like someone demented, and lost no time passing the information on to her solemn husband, who decided that, Hymen being in such a sad and sorry state, it could not under any circumstance be offered to the priests of Themis. These gentlemen, he pointed out, never joked about matters of such importance, and he was concerned lest his poor little sister-in-law find herself no sooner arrived in the town where "the scaffold was constantly ready and waiting" than she would perhaps be made to climb upon it and offered up as a victim to modesty and decency. The marquis cited chapter and verse—after dinner, especially, his erudition had a tendency to show itself—proving that the natives of Provence were indeed the descendants of an Egyptian colony; he noted that the Egyptians were very often given to sacrificing young girls, and that a presiding judge of the Aix court, who from an ancestral point of view was no more than an Egyptian colonist, could without any stretch of the imagination arrange to have the prettiest neck in the world, namely his dear sister's, separated from the rest of her body . . . Head choppers, these colonial magistrates; they can slice a neck, d'Olincourt went on, quicker than a crow can say "caw," whether for good reason or not concerns them not one whit. Like Themis, inflexibility wears a bandage over its eyes, placed there by stupidity; and in a town like Aix philosophy never sees fit to remove it . . .

It was therefore decided to hold a meeting: the count, the marquis, Madame d'Olincourt, and her charming sister went to dine at a modest house the marquis owned in the Bois de Boulogne, and there the stern Areopagus decided, in an enigmatic style reminiscent of the answers given by the Cumaean Sybil,[4] or of the decrees rendered by the Court of Aix (which, by virtue of its Egyptian origins, has certain claims to the use of hiero-glyphics), that the good judge should indeed be "wed and yet not wed."

The sentence having been passed, and the actors clearly rehearsed as to their roles, the group returns to the baron's house, where the young lady in question offers her father no opposition. D'Olincourt and his wife are, they assure, delighted about such a well-suited marriage; they insinuate themselves to an astonishing degree into the judge's good graces, are very careful not to laugh whenever he appears, and so worm their way into the hearts of both future son-in-law and father-in-law that they both readily consent to celebrate the mysteries of Hymen at the Château d'Olincourt not far from Melun, a magnificent estate belonging to the marquis. Everyone approves of the plan; only the baron offers his regrets at being unable to attend such a lovely celebration, but he will, he says, come and pay them a visit there if he can.

The day arrives at last, the happy couple is joined in holy matrimony at the Saint-Sulpice Church, in an early morning service, without any great to-do, and that very same day they set out for d'Olincourt. Count d'Elbène, bearing the name and in the garb of one La Brie, the marquis's personal valet, receives the group when it arrives, and, when the evening meal is over, escorts the newlyweds to the bridal chamber, whose furnishings and machinery he has arranged and for whose operation he has been made fully responsible.

"Verily, my pretty one," said the amorous native of Provence as soon as he found himself alone with his wife-to-be, "your charms are those of Venus herself, *capista!** I don't know where you got them, but one could scour the length and breadth of all Provence without finding anything to match them."

Saying which, he began to caress the poor little Téroze through her many layers of petticoats, while she tried to make up her mind whether to laugh or be frightened.

"May the Good Lord above damn me here and now," he went on, his hands roaming hither and thither, "and may I never judge another whore if these are not the shapes of love itself concealed beneath her mother's glittering petticoats."

Just then La Brie entered the room bearing two gold goblets, one of which he offered to the bride, the other to Monsieur de Fontanis.

"Drink, chaste couple," he said, "and may you both find the presents of love and the gifts of hymen in this drink. Your Honor," said La Brie when the good judge had seen fit to inquire about the reason for this drink, "this is a Parisian custom whose origins date back to the baptism of Clovis. It is a custom among us that, before celebrating those mysteries which will shortly occupy you both, you should partake of this potion which has been blessed by the bishop and receive therefrom the strength necessary for the undertaking."

"Ah, *parbleu!*"[5] cried the man of law, "I should be only too happy to observe the custom. Let me have the goblet, my friend, hand it to me . . . But, be forewarned,

---

*A Provençal swearword.

if you set a match to the wick, there's no telling what your young mistress may have to contend with; I'm already chafing at the bit, and if you push me past the breaking point, I can no longer be held responsible for my actions."

The judge drank up, his young bride followed suit, the valet withdrew, and the couple climbed into bed. But no sooner were they abed than the judge was stricken with such acute intestinal pains, with a need so urgent to relieve his frail nature on the side opposite from that which ought to have been seeking release, that, without the slightest regard for where he was, without the slightest respect for the fair person who was sharing his couch, he flooded the bed and the surrounding area with such a deluge of bile that the terrified Mademoiselle de Téroze barely had time to jump out of bed and call for help. Help came; Monsieur and Madame d'Olincourt, who had been careful not to go to bed, hurriedly arrived; the judge, dismayed beyond description, draped the sheets around himself in an effort to hide, not realizing that the more he tried to conceal himself the filthier he was becoming, until at last he was the object of such horror and disgust that his young wife, and the other people present, withdrew with loud protestations of pity over his condition and assurances that the baron would be informed of the matter without a minute to lose, so that he could dispatch forthwith one of the best doctors in Paris to the château.

"O Merciful Heaven," cried the poor appalled judge, as soon as he was alone, "what a fine kettle of fish this is! I thought it was only in our royal palace, and on the fleur-de-lis itself, that one could overflow in this manner; but on one's wedding night, in the wench's own bed, that I must confess I cannot conceive."

A lieutenant in d'Olincourt's regiment whose name was Delgatz and who, in order to take care of the medical needs of the regiment's horses, had taken two or three courses at the veterinary school, duly arrived the following morning in the guise of, and heralded as, one of the most famous disciples of Asclepius. It had been suggested to Monsieur de Fontanis that he appear in his most casual attire, and Madame de Fontanis—who in point of fact we ought not yet refer to by this name— went out of her way to tell her husband how attractive she found him in this outfit: he was wearing a dressing gown of pale yellow, with red stripes down to the waist, adorned with facings and lapels, beneath which he wore a little waistcoat of rough brown muslin, with sailor's breeches of a matching color and a red wool bonnet: all of this, enhanced even more by the interesting pallor caused by his accident of the night before, overwhelmed Mademoiselle de Téroze with such a wave of renewed love that she refused to leave his side for a quarter of an hour.

"In God's truth,"[6] said the judge. "The girl does love me. Truly, she is the woman heaven has sent to make me happy. I acted very badly last night, but it isn't every day one has an attack of diarrhea."

At length the doctor arrived, took his patient's pulse, and, expressing surprise at how weak he found him, proved to him by aphorisms culled from Hippocrates and commentaries from Galen that unless he fortified himself at dinner that evening with half a dozen bottles of Spanish and Madeira wine, he would find it impossible to manage the deflowering he had in mind. As for the attack of indigestion he had suffered the evening before, he assured him it was nothing.

"That attack, my dear sir," he said to him, "was a direct result of a failure on the part of the liver's ducts to filter the bile properly."

"But," said the marquis, "the accident was not dangerous."

"I beg to differ with you, Monsieur," the disciple of Epidaurus's temple[7] replied with great solemnity, "in medicine we have no minor causes which cannot become major unless they are arrested immediately by the profundity of our science. This minor accident might very well lead to a considerable change in Monsieur's organism. This unfiltered bile, borne by the arch of the aorta into the sub-clavicular artery, and thence transported by the carotids into the delicate membranes of the brain, could very well have produced madness by altering the circulation of animal spirits and suspending their natural activity."

"Oh, Heavens!" cried Mademoiselle de Téroze, bursting into tears. "My husband mad! Did you hear that, sister, my husband mad!"

"Please set your mind at ease, Madame. Thanks to the dispatch with which I have dealt with the problem, there is nothing to worry about, and I can now assure you the patient is on the road to recovery."

With these words, joy was seen to return to every heart; the Marquis d'Olincourt tenderly embraced his brother-in-law, showed in a lively and provincial manner how profoundly interested he was in his welfare, and pleasure was, once again, the sole order of the day.

That same day, the marquis having invited his vas-
sals and neighbors, the judge expressed a desire to deck
himself out in proper attire for the occasion. They kept
him from doing so, however, and reveled in the pleasure
of introducing him in that same bizarre attire to the entire society of the region.

"But he is so charming like that," the wicked marquise was saying at every opportunity. "Truly, if I had
known before I met you, Monsieur d'Olincourt, that the
sovereign magistrature of Aix included such amiable
gentlemen as my dear brother-in-law, I swear to you that
I would never have chosen a husband other than from
among that august and respected body."

The judge thanked her; he bowed and scraped with
a grating laugh, occasionally simpering in front of the
mirror, muttering to himself, "There's no denying it, old
boy, you're not bad, not bad at all."

At length the evening meal was announced. The
conspirators had invited the pseudo-doctor to stay over
and, as he himself drank like a fish, he had little trouble
persuading his patient to follow his good example. They
had been careful to place within close reach of the two
men some especially heady wines which, very quickly
befuddling the organs of their brains, soon put the judge
into the state they desired. The guests arose; the lieutenant, after his superb performance, retired to bed and
disappeared the following day. As for our hero, his dear
little wife took him in hand and led him toward the nuptial bed, escorted in triumphant procession by the entire
company. The marquise, whose usual charming self was
made even more so when she had imbibed a bit of champagne, told the judge she was sure that he had over-

indulged and that she was very much afraid that, over-heated by the fumes of Bacchus, he would once again remain unfettered by love's bonds that night.

"Don't fret about it for a single moment, Marquise," the judge replied. "These beguiling gods are, when joined together, but more formidable. As for reason, what does it matter—assuming one can manage very well without it—whether one loses it in wine or in the flames of love? What does it matter whether one has sacrificed it to one or the other of these twin divinities? As far as we judges are concerned, reason is the one thing in the world we manage to do without most easily: we banish it from our tribunals as we do from our heads; we make a sport of riding roughshod over it. This is what makes our decrees such masterpieces, for, although they are completely devoid of common sense, we carry them out as resolutely as though we knew precisely what they meant. As I live and breathe," the judge went on, stumbling slightly and stooping to pick up his red wool bonnet, which a moment's loss of equilibrium had separated from his hairless head, "yes, indeed, as I live and breathe, I declare without fear of false modesty that I am one of the best legal minds in my troop. It was I who last year talked my learned colleagues into exiling from the province for a period of ten years—and thereby ruining forever—a nobleman who had already served his king faithfully and well. And all that over a party of females.[8] They resisted, I kept on arguing, and the flock eventually came round to my way of seeing things . . . Goodness, I love morality, don't y'know, I love temperance and sobriety. Anything that offends these twin virtues is anathema to me, and I deal with it accordingly. One must

be severe, severity is the daughter of justice . . . and justice is the mother of . . . of . . . I beg your pardon, Madame,
there are times when I sometimes suffer a slight lapse of
memory . . ."

"Yes, indeed, you are quite right," replied the mad
marquise as she withdrew, taking the rest of the company
with her. "Only do take care that there are no further
lapses tonight such as those memory lapses you mention.
For we must finally bring this matter to a conclusion, and
my little sister—who worships you—cannot be expected
to put up with such abstinence forever."

"Have no fear, Madame, have no fear," the judge
went on, making an effort to accompany the marquise
with a step that can only be described as slightly un-
steady, "you may set your mind at ease. I shall return her
to you tomorrow as Madame de Fontanis, and that I
swear to you as surely as I am a man of honor. Isn't that
true, my dear?" the man of law continued, coming back
to his companion, "Don't you agree that tonight will see
our mission successfully accomplished? You can see how
much everyone wishes it; there is not a single member of
your family who is not honored to be united with me by
marriage; there's nothing more flattering for a household
than to have a judge as one of its members."

"Who can say you nay, Monsieur," the young lady
answered. "I can only assure that, speaking personally, I
have never felt as proud as when I have heard myself referred to as 'the judge's wife.'"

"I can easily believe it. Come now, get undressed,
my turtle dove, I feel myself growing a trifle heavy, and I
should like to have done with our little business if possible before I fall completely asleep."

But as Mademoiselle Téroze—as is often the case with young brides—took forever primping and preparing herself for the nuptial bed: she could never find quite what she needed, was forever scolding her maids, and simply could not seem to finish; the judge, who had had his fill of waiting, decided to climb into bed, and from there he spent the next quarter of an hour calling out to her:

"Come on, *parbleu*, hurry up now! I can't understand what can be taking you so long. If you don't come soon it will be too late!"

In spite of his pleas, however, nothing happened, and since, given the state of drunkenness our modern Lycurgus[9] was in it was rather difficult to find one's head on a pillow without falling asleep thereon, he yielded to the most urgent of needs and was already snoring, as though he had just finished sentencing some Marseilles whore, before Mademoiselle de Téroze had even slipped out of her chemise.

"Fast asleep!" said Count d'Elbène as he tiptoed into the room. "Come, my love, come and grant me the happy moments this coarse beast wanted to steal from us."

So saying, he spirited away with him the beloved object of his affection. The lights were extinguished in the bridal chamber, whose floor was immediately covered with mattresses. At a given signal, that part of the bed occupied by our man of the long robe was separated from the rest and, by means of a system of pulleys, raised to a height of twenty feet without our legal warrior, because of his inebriated state, ever being one whit the wiser.

At about three in the morning, however, wakened by

a slight fullness of the bladder, and remembering that he had seen a night table containing the chamber pot necessary to relieve it, he reached out for it; at first surprised to find nothing but emptiness around him, he groped further; but the bed, which was suspended only by the ropes, responded in accordance with the movements of the person leaning out of it and, eventually passing the point of no return, tipped completely over, spilling out the load wherewith it was charged into the middle of the room.

The judge tumbled onto the mattresses that had been prepared for him, and so great was his surprise that he began to bellow like a calf being led to slaughter.

"What the devil's going on here!" he said to himself. "Madame, Madame! I assume you're not far off, in which case will you kindly explain to me what this fall is all about? Last night I went to bed no more than four feet above the floor, and all of a sudden, while reaching for my chamber pot, I fell more than twenty!"

But since no one responded to these tender laments, the judge, who when all was said and done was not all that uncomfortable where he was lying, forsook his efforts to find out what had happened and spent the rest of the night there, as though he were in his lowly bed in Aix.

After the judge had fallen, our friends had been careful to gently lower the bed which, fitting snugly back into the part from which it had been separated, seemed once again to be part and parcel of the same marriage couch. At about nine o'clock in the morning, Mademoiselle de Téroze tiptoed back into the room. As soon as she was inside, she opened all the windows and rang for her maids.

"I must tell you, Monsieur," she said to the judge, "that your company is not exactly what I would call pleasant, and I can assure you that I intend to complain to my family about the way you have been treating me."

"What do you mean?" said the judge, coming to his senses and rubbing his eyes, still totally in the dark as to the accident that had landed him on the floor.

"What do you mean, what do I mean!" said his young wife, thoroughly enjoying her husband's discomfiture. "Last night when I came over to you, impelled by the sentiments that perforce must bind me to you, hoping to receive assurances from you of the same sentiments, you pushed me away with repugnance and threw me onto the floor! . . ."

"Oh, Good Lord!" said the judge. "Listen, my pet, I think I'm beginning to understand what happened . . . I offer you my most profound apologies. Last night, when I awoke with a rather urgent need, I did everything I could to relieve it, and in my thrashing about I not only threw myself out of bed but must have kicked you out as well. Besides which, the other extenuating circumstance is that I was most certainly dreaming, for I thought I had fallen from a height of twenty feet. Come, come, my angel, it's nothing, nothing at all. We shall merely have to postpone our little game until tonight, and I promise you that I shall remain as sober as a judge. I shall drink nothing but water. But at least give me a kiss, my sugarplum, let's kiss and make up before we face the others, or else I shall be quite convinced that you are holding a grudge against me, and that I wouldn't want for all the world."

Mademoiselle de Téroze consented to offer one of her cheeks, still flushed from the flames of love, to the foul kisses of the old satyr. The company came into the bedchamber, and both husband and wife carefully concealed the unfortunate catastrophe of the previous night.

The entire day was spent in pleasurable activities, the most notable of which was a long walk that took Monsieur de Fontanis away from the château and gave La Brie sufficient time to prepare some new settings. The judge, now bound and determined to consummate his marriage, was so fastidious during meals that it became impossible to utilize these means to unseat his reason, but fortunately our friends had more than one trump card up their sleeves, and the worthy Fontanis had too many sworn enemies to be able to escape from the traps they had set for him.

Again the company got up to go to bed.

"Ah, tonight, my angel," said the judge to his younger half, "I flatter myself that you will not get away again scot-free."

But even as he was thus blustering and bragging, the arm he was threatening to use was far from being in a state of readiness, and since he did not want to appear unprepared on the field of battle, the poor Provençal began exercising in a most incredible fashion in his own corner . . . He stretched out, he made himself as stiff as possible, every nerve in his body as taut as could be . . . all of which, causing him to exert double or treble the pressure on his bed that he would have exerted in a state of repose, finally broke the beams of the floor below, which had been previously sawed almost all the way through, and tossed the hapless magistrate head over heels into a pigsty which just happened to be directly below his room.

For a long time thereafter the company assembled at the Château d'Olincourt argued over who must have been the more surprised—the judge upon finding himself thus among animals so common in his part of the country, or the animals upon seeing one of the most famous judges of the High Court of Aix land in their midst. There were those who maintained that the satisfaction must have been mutual: in fact, mustn't the judge have been in seventh heaven to find himself, as it were, once again in good company, to breathe for a moment the tang of the good earth? And, for their part, mustn't those animals that the blessed Moses proclaimed impure have thanked their lucky stars to find at long last a judge not only in their midst but at their head, and, what is more, a judge of the High Court of Aix who, accustomed from childhood to ruling on causes relating to these beasts' favorite element, might one day arrange and forestall any discussion bearing upon this element so analogous to the organization of both parties?

Be that as it may, given the fact that introductions were not immediately forthcoming and that civilization, the mother of good breeding, is scarcely any more advanced among the members of the High Court of Aix than it is among the animals whom the children of Israel eschew, there was an initial moment of shock, during which the judge won no laurels: he was beaten, bruised, and battered from pillar to post by the snouts of the pigs. He admonished them, to no avail; he promised to enter their grievances in the record book, but again they turned a deaf ear to his words; he spoke of decrees, they remained just as unimpressed; he threatened them with exile, they responded by trampling him underfoot; and the star-crossed Fontanis, who by then was bloody but unbowed, was already in the process of preparing a sentence which was nothing less than burning at the stake when help finally reached him.

It was La Brie and the good colonel of dragoons who, armed with flaming torches, came to try to extricate the magistrate from the muck in which he was mired. But the question remained: by what part of him could one safely grab hold? For as he was generously and duly garnished from head to foot, it was not very easy to get hold of him, and the stench was overwhelming. La Brie went off to fetch a pitchfork, a hastily summoned stableboy brought another, and thus wise did they haul him, as best they could, out of the unspeakable muck into which he had fallen and been buried . . .

But now the next difficulty arose, and it was not an easy one to solve: having extricated him, where should they take him? They discussed purging the decree, the guilty would have to be cleansed; the colonel suggested letters of annulment, but the stableboy, who did not understand a word of these high-blown phrases, said that they would quite simply have to put him for a couple of hours into the watering trough; after that he would be sufficiently soaked for them to finish the job of prettifying him with handsful of straw. But the marquis declared that the cold water would most certainly affect his brother-in-law's health. Hearing which, and having ascertained that the kitchen boy's scullery was still filled with hot water, La Brie and the others carried the judge into the kitchen and turned him over to this disciple of Comus, who in no time at all had made him as spick-and-span as a china bowl.

"I suggest that you might be well advised not to go back to your wife tonight," said d'Olincourt as soon as he saw the cleanly scrubbed man of the law. "I know how fastidious you are; therefore La Brie here is going to take you to some modest bachelor's quarters where you can spend the rest of the night in peace."

"Good, good, my dear Marquis," said the judge. "I approve of your plan . . . But you have to admit that I must be bewitched to have such adventures happen to me every night since my arrival in this accursed castle."

"There is surely some physical explanation for all this," said the marquis. "The doctor's coming back to see us tomorrow. I suggest that you ask him about it."

"I will indeed," replied the judge and, repairing to his modest room in the company of La Brie, said to him as he climbed into bed: "The truth, my friend, is that before all this happened I was within a cat's whisker of attaining the goal."

"Alas, Monsieur," replied the clever fellow, as he was about to leave the room, "the finger of fate is clearly discernible in these acts, which are decreed in heaven, and I can only assure you that I pity you with all my heart."

After Delgatz had taken the judge's pulse, he assured him that the beams had broken simply due to an excessive blockage of the lymphatic vessels, which doubled the weight of the humors and proportionately increased the animal volume. As a result, a strict diet would have to be imposed which, after it had succeeded in purging the acridity of the humors, would necessarily reduce the physical weight and contribute to the success of the proposed venture which, as a matter of fact . . .

"But, Sir," Fontanis broke in, "this frightful fall has left me with a dislocated hip and a sprained left arm . . ."

"I believe every word you say," the doctor replied, "but these secondary accidents are not at all what worries me. My personal concern is always to trace things back to their sources. It's a matter of the blood, Monsieur; by diminishing the acrimoniousness of the lymph, we relieve the vessels, and since the circulation of the vessels becomes increasingly free we necessarily diminish the physical mass, and as a result ceilings no longer collapse beneath your weight and you will henceforth be able to devote yourself to whatever bed games you may choose to indulge in without any further fears of subsequent dangers."

"And what about my arm, Monsieur? And my hip?"

"Let us purge, Monsieur, the answer is to purge. After which let us proceed to a couple of localized bleedings, and everything will little by little return to normal."

That very same day the diet was started. Delgatz, who did not leave his patient's side throughout the entire week, kept him on a strict diet of chicken broth, and purged him three times running, all the while forbidding him above all to think about his wife. However lacking in medical skills, Lieutenant Delgatz's diet worked wonders, and he confided to the assembled company that he had once treated in like manner, when he had worked at the school of veterinary medicine, an ass who had fallen into a very deep hole, and that by the end of the month the animal was carrying its bags of plaster just as it had always done. And in fact, the judge, who could not help being bilious by nature, soon had a tad of color back in his cheeks; the bruises disappeared, until the concern of

everyone was to restore him to perfect health again and
to instill in him the forces required for him to claim what
was still rightfully his.

During the twelfth day of treatment, Delgatz took
his patient by the hand and, presenting him to Mademoiselle de Téroze, said:

"Here he is, Madame, here is this man upon whom
the laws of Hippocrates seem to have little or no effect. I
return him to you safe and sound, and if he gives free
rein to the forces which I have restored to him, we shall
have the pleasure of seeing before six months is out"—at
this point Delgatz placed his hand lightly on Mademoiselle's lower abdomen—"yes, Madame, we shall all have
the satisfaction of seeing this lovely womb rounded by
the hand of Hymen."

"May the Good Lord hearken to your words, Doctor," replied the saucy young thing. "You must admit that
it is indeed difficult to be a wife for the past fortnight
without at the same time having ceased to be a virgin."

"Incredible," said the judge. "It is not every night
that one suffers from indigestion, nor is it every night
that the desire to urinate precipitates a husband head
over heels out of his bed, or that, firmly believing he is
falling into the arms of a lovely woman, he is tossed
helter-skelter into a pigsty."

"We shall see," said the young Téroze with a deep
sigh, "we shall see, Monsieur. But if you loved me as I
love you, I am sure that all these misfortunes would not
have befallen you."

Supper was marked by great joviality; the marquise
showed herself at table to be both gracious and wicked:
she wagered against her husband that her brother-in-law

would that night cull the fruits of Hymen, and on this note everyone retired.

Both husband and wife made short shrift of their toilets. Out of modesty, Mademoiselle de Téroze begged her husband not to allow any light on in her bedchamber; he, too subdued by previous events to argue the point, readily agreed, and they climbed into bed. There were no further obstacles, and at long last the judge triumphed: he plucked, or thought he plucked, that precious flower to which mankind so foolishly attaches such importance. Five times in a row were his amatory efforts crowned with success.

With the break of day, the curtains were drawn back, and the rays of the sun that streamed through the windows revealed at last to the eyes of the victor the victim that he had just sacrificed on the altar of love . . .

Good Heavens! Imagine what must have been his reaction when he perceived an elderly black woman instead of his wife, when he saw a face as dark as it was ugly in the place of the delicate charms of which he had till that moment thought himself the possessor! He flung himself back, cried out that he was almost certainly a victim of some strange witchcraft, and at that moment his wife entered the room and, finding him with this divine creature from Cape Taenarus,[10] asked him tartly what she had done to him that might explain such a cruel betrayal.

"But, Madame, wasn't it with you yesterday that I . . ."

"However humiliated and ashamed I may feel, Monsieur, I have never been lacking in obedience to you, on that score my conscience is clear. You saw this woman beside me, pushed me roughly aside in order to lay hands on her; you then gave her my place—my rightful place—in bed, and I, by this thoroughly bewildered, left the room with only my tears to comfort me."

"And, if you do not mind my asking, my angel, are you quite sure that all these allegations are in fact true?"

"Oh, the monster! He dares to heap insult on injury, and when I have every right to expect amends all I get are sarcastic remarks . . . Help! Help! Sister! I want my whole family to come and see the unworthy object for whom I have been sacrificed . . . Look at her! There she is! There is that hateful rival," shouted the young wife who had been denied her rights, loosing a flood of tears. "He even dares to hold her in his arms right here in my presence. O my friends," Mademoiselle de Téroze went on, gathering everyone around her, "I beg you to help me, lend me arms wherewith to do battle against this false-hearted knave, this perjurer! Is this what I had a right to expect, adoring him as I did . . ."

Nothing could have been more comical than Fontanis's face when he heard these astonishing words. Now and then he would cast a distraught look at his black lady-friend, only to bring his gaze back again to his young wife, at whom he would stare with a kind of idiotic fixation that might truly have become a cause for concern as to the state of his brain.

By one of those curious strokes of fate, the person in whom the judge had come to place the most confidence since his arrival at the Château d'Olincourt was the very man he should have feared the most, his rival La Brie. He summoned him.

"My friend," he said to him, "you have always

struck me as a level-headed young fellow. Would you be kind enough to tell me whether or not you have noticed any change in my brain?"

"Upon my word, Your Honor," La Brie replied with a woebegone air, his face betraying his embarrassment, "I would never have dared to say anything to you, but since you have done me the honor of asking my opinion, I must confess that since you fell into the pigsty the ideas that have emanated from the membranes of your brain have been something less than pure. But don't let this bother you, Sir: the doctor who has already treated you is one of the greatest men who has ever come from this part of the country . . . Why, I recall a judge we used to have here, a judge from the marquis's district, who had become so mad that nary a young libertine from the region could have a bit of fun with a girl without this rascal straightway accusing him and bringing him to trial, with decrees and sentences and exiles and all the other platitudes that are always on these jokers' lips. Well, Sir, our doctor—that man of many talents who has already had the honor of administering to you with eighteen bleedings and thirty-two different kinds of medicine—made him as sane as though he had never judged anyone in his whole life. But, as I live and breathe," La Brie went on, turning toward some sound he had just heard, "how apt is the saying, 'Speaking of the devil . . . ,' for here he is in person."

"Good morning, Doctor," said the marquise, seeing Dr. Delgatz arrive. "I must say, I believe that we have never been more in need of your ministrations. Last night our dear friend the judge suffered a slight mental aberration which caused him, in spite of everyone, to sleep with this black woman instead of his wife."

"In spite of everyone?" said the judge. "You mean to say someone tried to stop me?"

"I for one, with every ounce of strength at my command," La Brie replied, "but Monsieur was going at it tooth and nail, so that I preferred to let him proceed rather than expose myself to the risk of being manhandled by him."

Hearing this, the judge began to scratch his head, and was no longer quite certain what to believe, when the doctor came over and took his pulse.

"This is more serious than the previous accident," said Delgatz, lowering his eyes. "This is some unknown vestige of our last illness, a banked fire which eludes the scientist's sharp eye and breaks into flame when one least expects it. There is a decided blockage in the diaphragm, and a tremendous erethical condition of the organism."

"A heretical condition!" cried the judge, beside himself with anger. "Just what does this joker mean by his 'heretical condition'? I want you to know, you cad, that I have never been a heretic. It is easy to see, you blockhead, that, with little or no knowledge of French history, you are completely unaware of the fact that *we* are the ones who burn the heretics. Go and visit our part of the country, you forgotten bastard from Salerno, go, my friend, go and see Mérindol and Cabrières still smoking from the fires that we caused to be set there, take a stroll on the rivers of blood with which the worthy members of our tribunal so generously water the earth of the province, you can still hear the moans of the poor wretches whom we have sacrificed to our rage, the sobs of the women whom we tear from their husbands' arms, the cries of the children whom we crush on their mothers' breasts; take a long, careful look at all the holy horrors that we committed, and then let me know whether a rascal like you has any right to accuse us of being heretics!"

The judge, who was still in bed beside his dark-skinned lady-friend, had grown so excited in the course of his narration that he had unwittingly punched the poor woman right in the nose, causing her to flee from the room yelping like a bitch whose pups have been taken away from her.

"My, my, what a lot of sound and fury, my friend," said d'Olincourt, coming over to the patient. "My dear judge, is that any way to act? It must be obvious to you now that your health is in a state of flux, and that it is absolutely essential that we take care of you."

"That's more like it," said the judge. "When anyone speaks to me this way I am only too happy to listen, but to hear myself accused of being a heretic by this Hippocratic hack is, you must admit, more than I should be expected to bear."

"My dear brother," said the marquise graciously, "such was not his intent. He was referring to 'erethism,' which is a synonym for extreme irritation. At no time was he speaking of heresy."

"Oh, I beg your pardon, my dear marquise. The problem is that I am sometimes a trifle hard of hearing. Come, let bygones be bygones, and have this worthy disciple of Averroës[11] come over here and speak his piece, and I shall hear what he has to say. In fact, I shall do more: I shall follow whatever instructions he may give me."

Delgatz, who had stepped back in the course of the judge's boiling tirade for fear that he might receive the same medicine that the judge had meted out to his bed companion, returned once again to the edge of the bed.

"As I was saying, Monsieur," said the latter-day Galen, again taking his patient's pulse, "a serious erethical condition in the organism . . ."

"A hereti . . ."

"Erethism, Monsieur," the doctor said hastily, cringing for fear a punch was on the way, "which leads me to conclude that we should proceed with a quick phlebotimization of the jugular vein, to be followed by a series of ice-cold baths."

"I'm not sure that I agree with the bleeding," said d'Olincourt. "His Honor the judge is no longer of an age to resist this kind of assault unless the need is really great. In fact, I am not a particular partisan, following the example of Themis and Asclepius, of the sanguinary mania: my theory is that there are as few illnesses that are worth the trouble of causing blood to flow as there are crimes over which blood ought to be spilled. My dear judge, I hope you will approve of what I say when it is a question of sparing your own blood; perhaps you would be less prone to agree if your interest in the problem were less immediate."

"Monsieur," the judge replied, "I approve of what you say in the first part of your statement, but I trust you will not take offense if I take exception to the second. 'Tis by blood that crime is obliterated, with blood alone that it can be purged and prevented. I only ask you, Sir, to compare all the evil that crime can bring forth with the minor misfortune of a dozen or so poor wretches executed per year in order to prevent it."

"Your paradox is lacking in common sense, my friend," d'Olincourt said. "It is inspired by a complete lack of flexibility, and by stupidity. There is in you a vice imputable both to the state and soil whence you spring, and you should foreswear it forever. Irrespective of the fact that your ridiculous strictness has never stopped a crime from being committed, it is perfectly absurd to maintain that one crime can pay for another, and that the death of a second person can in any way atone for another. You and your colleagues ought to blush with shame at such methods, which are far less a proof of your integrity than they are evidence of your overwhelming predilection for despotism. Those who call you the torturers and tyrants of the human race are absolutely right: you destroy, by yourselves, more men than all of Nature's plagues put together."

"Gentlemen," said the marquise, "it seems to be that this is neither the time nor place for such a discussion. Instead of calming my dear brother-in-law, Monsieur," she went on, turning to her husband, "you are merely inflaming his blood all the more, and if you keep on you may even turn his illness into something incurable."

"The marquise is right," said the doctor. "May I beg your leave, Monsieur, to ask La Brie to have forty pounds of ice brought in and put into the bathtub, which we shall then fill with well water. And while all these preparations are taking place, I shall help my patient get up."

With these words, everyone withdrew. The judge got up, haggled a trifle longer about the ice-bath which, he said, was going to make him good for nothing for at least six weeks. But all his arguments fell on deaf ears; they proceeded downstairs, and into the bath he went! They kept him there for ten or twelve minutes, in full view of the full company, who had gathered in every nook and cranny of the room to contemplate and savor the spectacle. After the patient had been thoroughly dried off, he dressed and rejoined the group as though nothing had happened.

As soon as dinner was over, the marquise suggested they go for a walk.

"The relaxation ought to be good for the judge, don't you think so, Doctor?" she asked Delgatz.

"Most certainly," he replied. "Madame doubtless remembers that no hospital worthy of the name fails to provide its inmates with a courtyard in which they can get a breath of fresh air."

"But I flatter myself," said the judge, "that you do not consider me completely dim-witted!"

"Very nearly, Monsieur," Delgatz went on. "This is a slight aberration which, caught in time, ought not to have any consequences. But what Your Honor requires is calm, and time to recuperate."

"What does that mean, Sir? Are you suggesting that I shall not be able to get my revenge tonight?"

"Tonight, Monsieur! The very thought makes me shudder. If I were to apply the same stern measures to you as you apply to others, I would forbid you from having anything to do with women for three or four months."

"Three or four months! Good heavens ... ," and, turning to his young bride: "Three or four months, my pretty one. Will you be able to hold out, my angel? Do you think you'll be able to wait that long?"

"Oh, Monsieur Delgatz will relent, I trust," the young Téroze replied with feigned naïveté. "He will at least take pity on me, if not on you ..."

And with these words they went for their walk.

In order to reach the house of a neighboring nobleman, who was privy to all that was going on and who was expecting the company for tea, they had to take a ferry. Once on the ferryboat, our young friends began to make merry, and Fontanis was quick to imitate them, in an effort to please his wife.

"Judge," said the marquis, "I'm willing to wager that you can't hang for several minutes from the ferryboat rope, the way I'm doing."

"Nothing could be simpler," said the judge, taking a pinch of snuff and standing up on his tiptoes in order to get a better grip on the rope.

"Excellent, excellent! Much better than you, my dear brother," said Mademoiselle de Téroze as soon as she saw her husband take hold of the rope.

But while the judge, thus suspended, called their attention to how graceful and skillful he was, the ferryman, who had been cued in to the plan, began to double his strokes, and the ferryboat literally sped away, leaving the poor fellow suspended between the heaven above and the water below ...

He cried out, he called for help; they were only about halfway across the river, with a good thirty yards more to go before they reached the bank.

"Do the best you can," they shouted to him, "you can make it to the bank by moving hand over hand. But you can see the wind is carrying us away, there's no way we can get back to you . . ."

Hearing which, the judge, slipping and sliding, flailing his legs, was struggling with all his might in an effort to catch up with the ferryboat, which the ferrymen by rowing deftly were careful to keep well ahead of him.

If ever there was an amusing sight, it surely must have been the sight of one of the most distinguished magistrates of the High Court of Aix thus suspended, in his long wig and black suit, over the flowing waters.

"Your Honor," the marquis cried out to him, "the truth of the matter is, this is nothing but an act of Providence: 'tis the *lex talionis*, my friend, which calls for an eye for an eye, a tooth for a tooth; that favorite law of your tribunals. What are you complaining about? At being strung up in this manner? But haven't you sentenced to the same torture others who did not deserve it any more than you?"

But by now the judge was beyond the reach of words. Terribly tired by the violent exertions he had been forced to make, the judge could hold on no longer; his hands slipped, and he fell like a rock into the water. At the same moment, two divers, who had been held in readiness, quickly swam to help him; they soon had him back onboard, as soaked as a spaniel and swearing like an old trooper. He began by berating them for their practical joke which, he said, was quite out of place . . . They swore to him that it was not at all a joke, that a gust of wind had caught the boat and carried it away. They hustled him into the ferryman's cabin, which was heated, and there his dear little wife coddled him and helped him change his clothes, doing everything she could to make him forget the little incident, until finally Fontanis, who was weak to begin with and in love to boot, began to laugh with all the others at the spectacle he had just made of himself.

At length they reached the neighboring nobleman's and were received with open arms. A magnificent high tea was served: care was taken to serve the judge a pistachio cream-cake which had no sooner made the journey to his entrails than he found himself compelled to ask, virtually in the next breath, where the toilet was. He was directed to one that was cloaked in darkness. In a frightful hurry, he sat down and relieved himself without further ado; but when he had finished, the judge discovered he could not get up.

"Now what the devil's this," he cried out, shaking his bottom . . . But try as he might, there was no way of breaking loose, short of leaving a bit of his bottom behind.

Meanwhile, his absence was noticed, causing a certain amount of concern and consternation. Everyone there began to ask one another what in the world could have become of him until, drawn by his shouts, they finally were drawn to the door of the fatal toilet.

"What the devil's keeping you in there so long, my friend?" d'Olincourt asked him. "Are you suffering from some kind of colic?"

"Colic, hell!" said the poor devil, redoubling his efforts to pry himself loose, "can't you see I'm stuck! . . ."

But in order to add a bit of spice to the spectacle,

and in order to make the judge squirm even more in an effort to pry himself loose from the damned seat, the group had someone stationed beneath the privy run a small flame from an alcohol burner over his buttocks, scorching the hair and upon occasion actually burning him, all of which made him jump and jerk and contort his face into horrible grimaces. The harder they laughed the more furious he became: he swore at the women and threatened the men, and the angrier he became the more comical his beet-red face was to behold. The various contortions he had made had managed to separate his wig from his head, and that bare skull made his facial contortions all the more comical.

At last their host arrived, embarrassed beyond words and begging the judge's pardon a thousand times over for not warning him that this toilet was in no condition to receive him. He and some of his servants managed to pry loose the long-suffering soul as best they could, but not without his leaving behind, as it were, a circular layer of flesh that remained attached to the ring of the seat which the painters had sized with a special glue in preparation for the paint with which they planned to decorate it. It is all well and good to say that man is well fleshed in these regions, but when it comes to leaving even an ounce or two behind it is another matter altogether.

"The truth is," said Fontanis, reappearing once again as bold as brass, "I'm a great asset to you all . . . but only as a butt for your jokes."

"Fair-weather friend," d'Olincourt rejoined, "why do you always have to blame us for misfortune which can only be rightly ascribed to the hand of fate? I always thought that the mere fact of donning Themis's halter was sufficient to make equity a natural virtue, but I can see that I was mistaken."

"That is because your ideas concerning what is called equity are unclear," said the judge. "In law we acknowledge several kinds of equity. There is what is called relative equity and personal equity . . ."

"Not so fast there," said the marquis. "I have never noticed that this virtue which is the object of so much analysis is very often practiced. What *I* call equity, my friend, is very simply the law of Nature. One is always just and upright when one follows it; one only becomes unjust when one deviates from it. Tell me, Judge, if you were to indulge in some whim of your imagination, within the safe confines of your own home, would you find it very equitable if a gang of roughnecks burst into your family hearth carrying torches and there, resorting to all kinds of mischievous and inquisitorial ruses, using bought information in an effort to ferret out some failings of which you may have been guilty when you were twenty or thirty, would try to take advantage of these atrocious methods to ruin you, to expel you from home and country, put an indelible blot on your escutcheon, dishonor your children and plunder your possessions: tell me, my friend, tell me honestly: would you find these scoundrels equitable?"[12]

"And judge it, may I ask? Do you mean to tell me you are blaming us for ferreting out crime! . . . It's our duty!"

"That is false, Sir: your duty consists only in punishing crime whenever it has been uncovered. Leave to the stupid and unrelenting maxims of the Inquisition the barbarous and tasteless task of ferreting out crime like vile spies and foul informers. What citizen can feel himself safe when, surrounded by servants you have been careful to bribe, his honor or his life will at any moment be in the hands of persons who, embittered by the chains they wear, think they can free themselves from them, or at least lighten their burden, by selling to you the man who imposes these chains upon them? What will you have accomplished? You will have increased manyfold the number of rogues and rascals in the State, you will have made God knows how many perfidious women, slandering servants, and ungrateful children: you will have doubled the sum of vices without having given birth to a single virtue."

"It is not a matter of giving birth to virtues; all we're concerned with is stamping out crime."

"But the means you use only multiplies it."

"Right you are! But that is the law, and we must follow it. We are not legislators, my dear marquis. My colleagues and I are simply *implementers*."

"I have a better term for it, Judge, a much better term," d'Olincourt retorted, warming up to his topic. "I say that you are rather the *executioners, the unworthy torturers*, who, naturally enemies of the State, derive your only pleasure from subverting its prosperity, from placing obstacles in the path of its happiness, sullying its glory, and causing the precious blood of its subjects to flow without rhyme or reason."

In spite of the two cold baths that Fontanis had taken that day, bile is something so difficult to destroy in a man of the long robe that the judge literally shook with rage to hear such aspersions being cast at a profession which he deemed so respectable. It had never crossed his mind that what is called the judiciary could be taxed with such charges, and he was perhaps on the verge of responding to the attack in the language of a sailor from Marseilles when the ladies came over and suggested that they start for home. The marquise asked the judge whether he needed to pay another visit to the water closet before they left.

"No, no, Madame," said the marquis. "This worthy magistrate does not always suffer from attacks of colic. You'll have to excuse him if he took this attack a trifle seriously. It is an illness of some consequence in Marseilles or Aix, this minor movement of the bowels. Ever since we have seen a troop of rogues—colleagues of our friend here present—judge that a few whores who were suffering from colic were *poisoned*, it should come as no surprise to us that colic is a serious matter indeed as far as a judge from Provence is concerned."

Fontanis, who in fact had been one of the most rabid judges in the case to which the marquis was referring, a case that had heaped shame upon the whole judicial body of Provence forever, was in a state difficult to portray: he stammered, he fussed and fidgeted, he frothed at the mouth, and in general resembled those mastiffs in a bullfight when they are unable to sink their teeth into their opponent. Whereupon d'Olincourt, taking advantage of the opportunity, said:

"Look at him, ladies, just look at him and tell me, I beg of you, whether you would look benevolently upon the fate of an unfortunate gentleman who, trusting in his innocence and good faith, should see fifteen mastiffs such as this one yapping at the seat of his trousers."

The judge was about to take serious umbrage at this remark, but the marquis, who did not want to create a scandal, at least not yet, having wisely repaired to his carriage, left to Mademoiselle de Téroze the task of smoothing over the wounds he had just inflicted. She was hard put to do so, but she finally succeeded in placating the judge.

The return trip on the ferry was without incident, the judge indicated no desire to dance beneath the rope, and the company reached the château without any further problem.

They had dinner, during which the doctor was careful to remind Fontanis of the necessity for him to eschew all contact with the fair sex.

"Upon my word," said the judge, "there is no need to warn me on that score. How do you expect a man who has spent the night with a dark-skinned lady he has never set eyes on before, who has been accused of being a heretic in the morning, has been made to take an ice bath for lunch, who shortly thereafter has fallen into the river, who, finding himself caught on the toilet, like a rat in a trap, has had his behind burnt to a crisp while he was peacefully moving his bowels, and who has been told to his face that judges who make an effort to ferret out crime are but sorry rogues and knaves, and that whores who have the colic are not whores who have been poisoned: how, I ask you, do you expect such a man to even entertain the idea of deflowering a virgin?"

"I am most pleased to see you so reasonable," said Delgatz, accompanying him to the little bachelor's quarters he occupied when he had no designs on his wife, "and I urge you to continue being so. If you do, you will soon feel the positive results."

The following day, the ice baths were repeated: during the entire time this treatment was in effect, the judge did not have to be reminded of the necessity to restrict his activities, and the lovely girl who was his wife and yet not his wife was at least able to take uninterrupted advantage, during this interval, of all of love's pleasures in the arms of her charming d'Elbène. At length, however, after two more weeks had gone by, Fontanis, once again feeling fit as a fiddle, began to pay court to his wife.

"Oh, really, Monsieur," this petite person said to him when she saw that further postponement was quite out of the question, "my mind is preoccupied with all sorts of matters other than love. Look at this letter I have just received, Monsieur. I'm ruined!"

Saying which, she handed her a husband a letter in which he read that the Château de Téroze, which was located four leagues from the château in which they were staying, in a little frequented section of the Fontainebleau Forest—it was the revenue from this estate that constituted his wife's dowry—had for the past six months been haunted. The ghosts living there, the letter went on, made a frightful noise, were harmful to the farmer, were causing the value of the land to decrease at an alarming rate—and unless something was done about it, neither the judge nor his good wife would ever touch a penny from it.

"This is terrible news," said the judge, handing back the letter. "But can't we ask your father to give us something other than this wretched castle?"

"And what do you suggest he give us, Monsieur? I must remind you that I am only a younger daughter. My father gave my sister a handsome dowry when she married. It would be unseemly for me to ask for something else; we must make do with what we have and try to put it to rights."

"But your father was fully aware of this shortcoming in the dowry when he gave you to me in marriage."

"I confess he did. But he did not believe the situation to be all that bad, and besides, this fact in no wise detracts from the value of the gift; it merely delays our reaping the benefits to be derived from it."

"And does the marquis know about this?"

"Yes, but he does not dare talk to you about it."

"He is wrong. It is quite clear that we must discuss the matter together as reasonable men."

D'Olincourt was summoned and, when asked, could only acknowledge that such indeed was the situation. The upshot of all this was that they mutually agreed that, despite whatever dangers the decision might present, the simplest solution was to repair to the château and spend two or three days there, to straighten things out and see just how much revenue could be salvaged from the property.

"Do you have a modicum of courage, Judge?"

"Me? That all depends," said Fontanis. "In our profession, courage is a virtue rarely required."

"I am fully aware of that," said the marquis. "All you need is ferociousness. The same goes for this virtue as for all the others: you know how to despoil them so thoroughly that you never take from them anything save that which spoils them."

"There you go again, Marquis, indulging in your sarcasms. Let us speak together as reasonable men, I beg of you, and save our spite for another time."

"All right, then, here is what we must do: we must go and spend a few days in the Château de Téroze, destroy the ghosts, straighten out the matter of income to be derived from your tenant farmer, and then come back and have you sleep with your wife."

"Just a moment, Monsieur, not quite so fast. Have you thought of the dangers involved if we start hobnobbing with such people? Proper proceedings, followed by a decree, would be a far better way of dealing with this whole matter."

"Here we go again with proceedings and decrees . . . Why don't you also excommunicate, the way the priests do? Atrocious weapons of tyranny and stupidity! When will all these cockroaches in their petticoats, all these cads in their morning coats, all these votaries of Themis and the Virgin Mary, stop thinking that their insolent prattle and ridiculous papers can have the slightest effect on the world? If you do not realize it already, Brother, let me remind you that 'tis not with scraps of paper such as these that one can hope to get the best of knaves as determined as these seem to be, but with swords, powder, and bullets. Make up your mind, therefore, either to die of hunger or to muster up the courage to fight them in this manner."

"My dear Marquis, you reason like a colonel of dragoons. Allow me to look at matters with the practiced eye of a man of law whose person, inviolate and of prime importance to the State, never exposes itself to danger without due and proper consideration."

"Your person of prime importance to the State, Judge! It's been a long time since I've had a good laugh, but I can see that you really want to inveigle a fit of laughter from me. Pray tell, how did you ever get the idea that someone generally of humble birth, an individual always in revolt against all the good that his master may desire, serving neither his purse nor his person, in constant conflict with all his good intentions, a person whose sole task is to foment division among private parties, to keep alive the divisiveness already abroad in the kingdom, to annoy and harass its citizens . . . how, I repeat, can you imagine that such a person can ever be 'important' to the State?"

"I refuse to become involved in any conversation where the other party merely wants to vent his spleen."

"All right, my friend, I agree: let's stick to the facts. If you were to spend a month thinking about this adventure, if you were ridiculous enough to ask your doddering old colleagues to give their opinion about it, I would still tell you that there is no other way of straightening out this problem save to go and take up residence in the very place where people are trying to do us in."

The judge continued to haggle, to defend his viewpoint by a thousand paradoxes each more absurd and more arrogant than the other, until at last he came to the same conclusion as the marquis, namely that they would both leave the following day, together with two footmen from the Château d'Olincourt. The judge, we have said, asked for La Brie, why God only knows, but he had a great deal of confidence in the boy. D'Olincourt, all too aware of the important matters that were destined to keep La Brie at the castle during their absence, replied that it would be impossible to take him, and the following day, at dawn, they made their preparations for departure. The ladies, who had risen for the purpose of seeing them off, outfitted the judge in an old suit of armor they had found in the castle. His young wife personally placed the helmet on his head, wished him all sorts of good luck, and bade him return with all due haste so as to receive from her hand the laurels he was going to cull. He embraced her tenderly, mounted his horse, and followed the marquis.

In spite of the fact that the people in the neighborhood had been forewarned of the masquerade that was due to pass by, the gaunt judge in his military accouterment looked so absolutely ridiculous that he was followed from one château to the next with bursts of laughter and hooting. His sole comfort was the colonel who, coming over to him from time to time, with a serious expression on his face, said to him:

"You see, my friend, the present world is but a farce. At times an actor, at times the audience, either we judge what is transpiring onstage or we find ourselves upon it."

"True. But on this one we are being booed," the judge said.

"You don't say?" the marquis replied phlegmatically.

"I do indeed," Fontanis retorted, "and you must admit it's hard to take."

"What!" said d'Olincourt. "You mean to tell me that you are not used to these minor disasters? Don't you realize that the public is also hooting at you each time you commit one of your stupidities from your lily-livered bench, emblazoned as it is with fleurs-de-lis?[13] Of course, since you, in your profession, are made to be scoffed at, dressed as you are in that grotesque manner that makes people laugh the moment they see you, how can you imagine that, with so many unfavorable things on one side, you will be forgiven your stupidities on the other?"

"You do not love the lawyer's robe, Marquis."

"I cannot say I do, Judge. I am only well disposed toward what is useful or pragmatic: any person whose only talent is to fabricate gods, or to kill men, seems to me a priori worthy only of public indignation, and ought to be either jeered at or sentenced to hard labor. Don't you think, my friend, that with the two excellent arms with which Nature has endowed you, you would be infinitely more useful behind a plow than perched on a bench in a court of justice? In the first instance you would do honor to all the faculties that you have received from Heaven, whereas in the second you but sully them."

"But you must admit the necessity of having judges."

"It would be far better to have naught but virtues, one could acquire them without judges; with judges, we run roughshod over them."

"And how do you expect a State to be governed? . . ."

"By three or four simple laws filed in the royal palace and upheld in each class by the elderly of that class. In such wise would each class have its peers, and it would not befall a gentleman who is accused to suffer the frightful shame of being judged and sentenced by scurvy fellows like you, who are so prodigiously far from being his equal."

"Oh, that is something we could argue about at great length . . ."

"Not at great length," said the marquis, "for here we are at the Château de Téroze."

They entered the château; the tenant-farmer appeared; he took the gentlemen's horses, and then they repaired to a room where they discussed the distressing things going on in the castle.

Every night a terrible noise could be heard throughout the house, without anyone being able to figure out where it was coming from. They had lain in wait; they had spent several nights in the house; several peasants in the employ of the tenant-farmer had, the story went, been badly beaten, and no one was any longer inclined to expose himself to further danger. But just what they suspected it was impossible to say. The rumor going round was, very simply, that the ghost was the spirit of a former tenant-farmer of this house who had had the misfortune to lose his life unjustly on the gallows, and who had sworn that he would come back every night and make a terrible din until he had the satisfaction of wringing the neck of a judge within the confines of this selfsame house.

"My dear Marquis," said the judge, reaching the door, "it seems to me that my presence here is rather useless. We are quite unaccustomed to this kind of revenge, and we, like doctors, prefer to kill indiscriminately whoever we so chose, without our having any trouble on the part of the deceased."

"Not so fast, Brother, not so fast," said d'Olincourt, stopping the judge, who was ready to leave. "Let us do this good man the honor of hearing him out." Then, turning to the tenant-farmer: "Is that all, Master Pierre? Haven't you any other details to pass on to us about this strange event? And does this spirit have a bone to pick with all judges in general?"

"No, Monsieur," Pierre replied. "The other day he left a written message on a table in which he said that he harbored no ill will against anyone save dishonest judges. Any honest judge has nothing to fear from him, but he will be unsparing with those who, motivated solely by despotism, stupidity, or a desire for revenge, have sacrificed their fellow man to the baseness of their passions."

"There, you can see that I must leave," said the judge with dismay, "there is no place in this house where I can feel sure of being out of harm's way."

"Ah, you scoundrel," said the marquis, "at long last your crimes are beginning to make you tremble in your boots. All the people you have disgraced, or sent into exile for ten years over a party of well-paid girls, all the base conniving with families of which you are guilty, the filthy lucre you have accepted in order to send some nobleman to his ruin, and all the other poor wretches sacrificed to your rage or ineptitude: these are the ghosts coming back to haunt you, are they not? What would you not give at present to have been an upright and honorable man all your life! May this cruel situation one day serve to teach you a lesson, may you realize beforehand how unbearable a weight is a guilty conscience and that there is not a single happiness in the world, no matter how great it may have seemed to us, that can compare to one's peace of mind and the profound pleasures of virtue."

"My dear Marquis," said the judge, with tears welling up into his eyes, "I beg your forgiveness. I am a ruined man. I beg you not to sacrifice me to these evil spirits, but rather allow me to return to your beloved sister, who is pining away waiting for me. She will never forgive you if you persist in subjecting me to such mischief."

"Coward! How right they are to say that cowardice always goes hand in hand with duplicity and treachery . . . No, you shall not leave; it's too late to turn back. My sister's only dowry is this castle. If you wish to take advantage of it, it must be purged of the rogues who are despoiling it. Vanquish or die: there is no middle ground."

"I beg to differ with you, my dear brother, but there *is* a middle ground, and that is to beat a quick retreat and give up all thought of deriving any profit from this property."

"Milksop! Is this how you show your love for my sister! You prefer to see her languish in poverty rather than fight to free her inheritance from the ghostly ties that bind it . . . Do you want me to tell her, when we get back, that these are the sentiments you proclaim!"

"Good Lord! To what terrible straits have I been reduced!"

"Come, come now, get a grip on yourself, and be prepared for whatever they may expect of us."

Dinner was served; the marquis insisted that the judge dine in his full suit of armor. Master Pierre joined them for dinner, and said that there was absolutely nothing to fear prior to eleven o'clock, but that from then until dawn the place was uninhabitable.

"And yet we shall not abandon it," said the marquis. "And here with me is a brave comrade-in-arms on whom

I count as I do on myself. I am positive he will not desert me."

"Don't count your chickens before they're hatched," said Fontanis. "I must confess that I'm a bit like Caesar. With me courage is like a woman: fickle and unpredictable."

Meanwhile, the time was spent in walking and surveying the surrounding area, and in going through the tenant-farmer's books. At nightfall, the marquis, the judge, and two servants repaired to the château.

The judge had a large room which looked directly onto two miserable towers, the very view of which was enough to make one shake in one's boots. According to all reports, it was from these towers, in fact, that the ghost began his rounds. Thus he was going to have a first crack at him. A man of courage would have been delighted at that happy prospect, but the judge, who like all judges everywhere in the world, but especially the judges of Provence, was anything but a man of courage, had such a cowardly reaction upon learning this piece of news that they were obliged to change his clothes from head to foot: never had any medicine acted more promptly. In spite of this, they dressed him again, suited him up in his garb of armor, put two revolvers on a table in his bedroom, placed a lance at least fifteen feet long in his hands, lighted three or four candles, and left him to his own devices.

"O you poor wretch, Fontanis," he cried as soon as he found himself alone, "what evil spirit has got you into such a scrape? Couldn't you have managed to find, in your own bailiwick, a girl as good as she, one who would not have given you all this trouble? But it was she you wanted, poor Judge, you set your cap for her, my friend, and look where it got you: you were tempted by the idea of a marriage in Paris and look at the results. . . . *Péchaire,** you may die here like a dog, without even having a chance to consummate your marriage, or giving up the ghost properly by receiving the last rites from a priest . . . These damned unbelievers, with their equity, their laws of Nature, and their munificence, they think that paradise ought to be opened up to them once they have pronounced these three lofty words . . . let us have less equity, less Nature, less charity: rather let us decree, let us exile, let us burn; let us break them upon the wheel and go to mass—'tis a far better system than all that other.

"This d'Olincourt seems passionately interested in the trial of the nobleman we sentenced last year. There must be some connection I didn't know about . . . But damn it, wasn't it a scandalous affair? Didn't a thirteen-year-old valet we bribed come and tell us, because we wanted him to tell us, that this poor fellow was murdering whores in his château? Didn't he come and tell us a Bluebeard kind of tale that no nanny would be caught dead relating to one of her charges? When we are dealing with a crime as momentous as the murder of a prostitute, an offense proven beyond any shadow of a doubt for the simple reason that you have the written deposition of a thirteen-year-old child whom we have had whipped with a hundred lashes because he didn't want to say what we wanted him to say, it seems to me that we did not act

---

*Another common Provençal oath.

with undue leniency when we decided to act as we did . . . Do you mean to tell me that we need a hundred witnesses to make certain a crime has been committed, when one informer ought to suffice? And what about our learned colleagues from Toulouse: did they have any such scruples when they had Calas broken on the wheel? If we were to punish only those crimes of which we are absolutely sure, we would have the pleasure of dragging our fellow men to the gallows no more than four times a century, and only by so doing do we manage to make ourselves respected. I should like someone to tell me what kind of a court we would have whose funds would be constantly available for the needs of the State, a court which would never remonstrate, which would record every edict and never kill anyone . . . I'll tell you what it would be: it would be a collection of dolts, the laughing-stock of the country . . . Don't lose heart, Judge, try and keep your pecker up: you only did what you had to do, my friend. Let the sworn enemies of the judiciary shout all they want, they will not destroy it. Our power, built upon the weakness of kings, will last as long as the empire; God's will, as far as kings are concerned, is that this power should not end up overthrowing them; a few more misfortunes like those that marked the reign of Charles VII can only lead to the ultimate destruction of the monarchy and its replacement by that republican form of government which, placing us on the pinnacle of power as was the Senate in Venice, will at least deliver into our hands the chains with which we are burning to grind down the people."

Such were the judge's ruminations when all of a sudden a terrible noise was heard simultaneously in all the rooms and corridors of the castle . . . The judge began to tremble in every fiber of his body; he clutched his chair; it was almost more than he could do to lift his eyes.

"I've completely lost my mind!" he shouted. "What business do I, what business does a judge of the High Court of Aix, have battling ghosts? Oh ye ghosts, I ask of you: what have you and the High Court of Aix ever had in common?"

And yet the intensity of the noise redoubled, the doors of the two towers burst open and terrifying figures entered the room . . . Fontanis dropped to his knees, begged that he be spared, that his life be spared.

"You scoundrel!" said one of these ghosts in a terrifying voice. "Was your own heart touched by pity when you wrongly condemned all those countless wretches? Did the frightful fate that was theirs have any effect on you? Were you any less vain or arrogant, less greedy or less dissolute the day your unjust decrees plunged the victims of your ridiculous inflexibility into misfortune, or into the grave? And where did you get the dangerous idea that your sudden power placed you above the law, or the illusive notion of your omnipotence that popular opinion lends for a moment or so and that philosophy just as quickly destroys? . . . Allow us to act in accordance with these same principles, and yield to our authority, since you are in no position to argue."

With these words, four of these physical spirits laid harsh hands on Fontanis and, in no time at all, stripped him as bare as the day he was born, without eliciting any other reaction from him than a flood of tears, a few screams, and an offensive layer of sweat that drenched him from head to foot.

"Now what shall we do with him?" said one of them.

"Wait," replied the ghost who appeared to be in charge. "I have here the list of the four principal murders that he has legally committed. Let us read them to him:

"In 1750 he sentenced to the wheel a poor wretch whose only crime had been to refuse him his daughter, whom the scoundrel wanted to seduce.

"In 1754, he offered to save a man's life in return for a payment of two thousand *écus;* since the man could not raise the sum, the judge had him hanged.

"In 1760, learning that a man in his town had made a few derogatory remarks about him, he sentenced him to be burned at the stake the following year as a sodomite, although this hapless creature had a wife and a whole host of children, all of whom gave the lie to his crime.

"In 1772, a young man of refinement who was a native of the region and who, as an act of good-natured revenge, wished to give a thorough drubbing to a courtesan who had given him a nasty present, had this practical joke turned into a serious crime by this unworthy churl, who treated the matter as a poisoning and attempted murder, talked all his colleagues into sharing his opinion, and thereby disgraced the young man, ruined him, and had him sentenced to death in absentia, since he had been unable to bring him bodily to trial.[14]

"These are his principal crimes. Make up your minds what to do with him, my friends."

Without a moment's delay a voice was raised: "The talion,[15] gentlemen, the law of retaliation. He has unjustly sentenced people to the wheel; I vote that he be broken on the wheel."

"I think he should be hanged," said another, "for the same reasons just given by my colleague."

"Let him be burned at the stake," said a third, "both because he dared use this torture when it was undeserved and because he himself has deserved it many times over."

"Let us show him an example of moderation and mercy, comrades," said the chief, "and let us use as the basis for our text for today the fourth adventure just related: a whipped whore is a crime worthy of death in the eyes of this silly blockhead; therefore let him be whipped himself."

Without further ado the poor judge was taken and placed facedown on a narrow bench, to which he was securely tied from head to foot. The four wanton spirits each took a leather thong five feet long and, striking up a cadence among them, proceeded to let the lashes fall with all the strength their arms could muster, on every square inch of poor Fontanis's bare body. After three quarters of an hour of uninterrupted lashing by the four vigorous hands to which his education had been entrusted, Fontanis's body began to look like one long welt from whose every nook and cranny blood was spurting.

"There, that's enough," said the chief. "As I said before, let's give him an example of pity and charity. If the shoe were on the other foot, the rascal would have us drawn and quartered. We have him at our mercy; I suggest we let him off with this brotherly punishment. We can only hope that this lesson at our school will teach him that murdering men is not the only way to make them better. All he received were five hundred lashes, but I'm willing to wager against all takers that he has changed his mind completely about injustice and that in the future he can be counted on to be one of the fairest magistrates of his profession. Untie him, and let us be off on our rounds."

"Great God!" the judge cried out, as soon as his torturers were gone. "I can see that if we hold up a torch to the actions of others, if we try to unfold them in order to have the pleasure of punishing them, yes, I can clearly see that in no time at all the chickens do come home to roost. And who in the world could have informed these people of everything I've done? How could they have been so well apprised of my conduct?"

Whatever the answer to that question, Fontanis tidied himself up as best he could; but no sooner had he slipped back into his clothes than he heard, emanating from the area toward which the ghosts had departed when they left his room, a series of blood-curdling screams. He strained his ear, and made out the voice of the marquis calling to him for help at the top of his lungs.

"I'll be damned if I respond," said the judge, who was completely exhausted. "Even if those rogues were to thrash him within an inch of his life, the way they did to me, I'd refuse to get involved. We all have our problems, and charity begins at home, I always say."

And yet the noise grew louder and louder, until finally d'Olincourt burst into Fontanis's room, with both his valets hard at his heels, all three of them screaming and yelping as though someone had just slit their throats. They were all covered with blood; one had his arm in a sling, the other's forehead was swathed in bandages, and

anyone who might have seen them thus—pale, di-
sheveled, and bloodied—would have sworn that they
had just done battle with a whole legion of devils, freshly
escaped from hell, in a knock-down-drag-out battle.

"Oh, my friend," said d'Olincourt, "what an assault!
I thought they were going to throttle all three of us right
here on the spot."

"I can assure you, you could not have been manhandled more than I," said the judge, showing his battered and bloodied backside. "Look what they did to me."

"Good Lord!" said the colonel of dragoons, "this
time the tables are turned, my friend, and you have
every reason to lodge a complaint. You are, I am sure,
well aware of the deep interest your colleagues have had
throughout the ages in whipped asses. Call a meeting of
the entire judiciary, my friend; find yourself some famous
lawyer who would be willing to lend his eloquence to the
defense of your molested buttocks. Utilizing the inge-
nious expedient whereby an orator in ancient times used
to move the Areopagus by uncovering, in the presence of
the court, the marvelous bosom of the beauty whose
cause he was pleading, let your Demosthenes choose the
most pathetic moment of his address to the court to lay
bare your much maligned buttocks, and thereby move
the tribunal to pity. Above all, remind the Paris judges
before whom you will be obliged to appear of that notorious incident in 1769[15] when, their hearts much more
moved to pity for the beaten backside of an ordinary
streetwalker than for the worthy people for whom they
feign the role of father and whom, nonetheless, they
allow to die of hunger, they decided to institute proceedings against a young officer who had just given the best

years of his youth to his sovereign and who, upon his return, found instead of laurels awaiting him naught but the humiliation prepared by the hands of the greatest enemies of that selfsame State which he had just defended . . .

"Come, my dear fellow-sufferer, let us not waste another moment, let us leave this accursed castle, for here there is not the slightest place where we can feel safe. Let us hurry and seek revenge, let us fly forthwith to the protectors of public order, the defenders of the oppressed, to the pillars of society, and ask for their help."

"I can't stand on my own two feet," said the judge, "and even if those damned scoundrels were to peel me again like an apple, I must beg of you to find me a bed and allow me to take to it for at least twenty-four hours."

"You can't be serious, my friend. You'll be strangled to death."

"Then so be it. It will be only one sin atoned for, and I must say that at present my heart is so filled with remorse that I would look upon any misfortune that might befall me as no more than an order from Heaven."

Since the commotion had completely subsided, and as d'Olincourt saw that the poor native of Provence was really in need of a little rest, he summoned good Master Pierre and asked him whether there was any danger of these scoundrels returning the following night.

"No, Monsieur," the farmer replied. "Tonight's activities will keep them quiet for the next eight to ten days, and you can go to bed without any concern on that score."

The badly crippled judge was taken to a room where he took to bed and rested as best he could for a good twelve hours. He was still fast asleep when suddenly he felt himself being inundated in his bed. He raised his eyes and saw the ceiling perforated with a thousand holes, from each of which there flowed a fountain with which he was threatened to be soaked unless he decamped as fast as his legs could carry him. He quickly dashed downstairs, completely naked, as best his backside permitted, where he found the colonel and Master Pierre seated around a dish of pâté and a battlement of Burgundy wine, wherewith they were drowning their sorrows. Their initial reaction, upon seeing Fontanis rush in clothed in such indecent dress, was to burst out laughing. The judge began to relate to them his latest woes; they made him sit down at the table, without giving him time to slip into his breeches—which he was still clutching under his arm much in the manner of the inhabitants of some primitive island. The judge began to drink, and by the time they had polished off the third bottle he found consolation for all his woes. Since by then only two hours remained before their scheduled departure for the Château d'Olincourt, they decided to have the horses saddled and to set off.

"That's some lesson you had me learn there, Marquis," said the judge as soon as they were in the saddle.

"And I can assure you it will not be the last, my friend," d'Olincourt replied. "Man is made to learn lessons, and especially men of law. 'Tis beneath the ermine-collared robe of jurisprudence that stupidity has erected its temple, and only in your tribunals can it breathe in total peace. But in any case, no matter what you might say, was it possible to leave this château before finding out what was going on there?"

"What good does it do us, now that we know?"

"For one thing it allows us to lodge our complaints now with a great deal more authority."

"Complaints! I'll be damned if I lodge any, thank you! I'll keep those I have to myself, and I'll be much obliged if you do the same."

"My dear friend, you are simply not consistent: if you find it ludicrous to lodge a complaint when one has been mistreated, why then do you go out of your way to look for them, why do you never stop provoking them? It makes no sense: you, who are one of crime's most ardent enemies, intend to let it go unpunished when it has been so clearly established? It is one of the most sublime axioms of jurisprudence, is it not, that, even assuming that the injured party waives his claim, justice still must demand its due? And are you not flying in the face of justice when you refuse to press your claims relative to what has just happened to you? Dare you refuse justice the rightful homage it demands?"

"You may be right on all scores, but I shall still not say a word."

"And what about your wife's dowry?"

"I shall count upon the baron's sense of fair play, and I shall ask him to take full responsibility for clearing up this matter."

"He will refuse to get involved."

"Then we shall live in poverty."

"What a gallant fellow! You'll be the cause of your wife's ruing the day she ever met you, of her bitterly regretting for the rest of her life that she ever cast her lot with a coward like you."

"Oh, as far as regrets are concerned, I suspect that

we shall each have our fair share. But pray tell me, why do you now want me to lodge a complaint, whereas nothing was further from your mind only minutes ago?"

"I didn't realize what was involved. As long as I thought we would be able to win without any outside help, I chose this method as the most honest. And now that I find it necessary to seek the assistance of the law I suggest it to you. What, may I ask, is inconsistent about that?"

"Marvelous, marvelous!" said Fontanis, climbing down off his horse as they were arriving at the Château d'Olincourt. "But still, I beg of you not to breathe a word of all this. That is the only favor I ask of you."

Although they had been gone for no more than two days, a great deal had transpired at the marquise's. Mademoiselle de Téroze was abed; a feigned indisposition, brought on by worry, by the sorrow of knowing that her husband was exposed to danger, had kept her in bed for the past twenty-four hours. A pretty bathing attendant was by her bed; her head and neck were swathed in twenty yards of gauze . . . a totally touching pallor, which made her a hundred times more beautiful than ever, rekindled all the fires of passion in the judge whose body was already further inflamed by the impassioned flogging he had just received.

Delgatz was at the patient's bedside, and in a low voice warned Fontanis not to manifest the slightest desire, given the unhappy situation in which his dear wife found herself. The critical moment had taken place during her periods; there was, he must be frank, a danger of losing her.

"Damnation!" said the judge. "I must have been

born under the most unlucky of stars. I have just been thrashed for this woman, and I mean thrashed within an inch of my life, and once again I am kept from claiming my rightful due from her!"

Moreover, the number of guests at the château had increased by three, and it is essential at this point to introduce the newcomers. Monsieur and Madame de Totteville, wealthy neighbors of the d'Olincourts, had just arrived with their daughter Lucille, a sprightly little brunette of about eighteen whose tender features were not one whit less lovely than those of Mademoiselle de Téroze. In order not to leave our readers in suspense any longer, we shall, without further ado, inform them who these three characters are whom we have deemed it appropriate to introduce at this juncture, either for the purpose of postponing the denouement or of leading the story more firmly to its desired conclusion.

Totteville was one of those impoverished knights of the order of Saint-Louis who, not above dragging their knighthood in the mire in exchange for a few free dinners or a handful of *écus*, accept indiscriminately whatever roles they are asked to play. His presumed wife was an old adventuress of another sort who, finding herself now at an age where she could no longer trade on her physical attractions, made up for it by dealing in the attractions of others. As for the lovely princess who was passed off as being their own flesh and blood, one can easily imagine, merely from her alliance with such a family, from what class she had come. A pupil of Paphos[16] from her most tender youth, she had already been the ruination of three or four farmer-generals, and it was because of her artfulness and beauty that they had adopted her. And yet all these characters, chosen from among the best their class had to offer, were well-schooled, perfectly instructed and, possessing the façade of good manners, performed to perfection what was expected of them, so much so that it was difficult, seeing them mingle with men and women of high society, not to believe that they too were members of it.

No sooner had the judge set foot in the door of the château than the marquise and her sister asked him for news of their adventure.

"It was nothing at all," said the marquis, respecting his brother-in-law's request, "merely a gang of scoundrels that we'll get the better of sooner or later. It's simply a matter of ascertaining what the judge's wishes are in the matter; we'll be only too happy to abide by them."

And as d'Olincourt had hastened to forewarn them in a whisper of the success of their mission and of the judge's desire that it not be discussed, they changed the subject and did not say another word about the ghosts of Téroze.

The judge told his wife how very concerned he was about her state, and said that what worried and upset him even more was the fact that her accursed ailment forced a further postponement of their moment of nuptial bliss. And as it was late, they dined and went to bed that day without further incident.

Monsieur de Fontanis, who as a worthy gentleman of the robe had in addition to his many other excellent qualities an excessive attraction for the fair sex, did not let the presence of young Lucille in the circle of the Marquise d'Olincourt go unnoticed. He began by asking his confidant, La Brie, who the young lady was; and La Brie, having replied in such a way as to encourage the seeds of love that he saw being planted in the judge's heart, persuaded him not to be backward.

"She's a girl from a fine family," the false-hearted confidant replied. "But that does not mean she is immune to a proposal of love from a man such as you. Your Honor," the young mischief-maker went on, "you are the scourge of fathers and the terror of husbands, and no matter what vows of fidelity a member of the fair sex may have made, it is extremely difficult to resist you. Forgetting for a moment the figure you cut, think of the position you hold: what woman can resist the allurements of a man of justice—that long black robe, that square judge's bonnet—do you think for a minute that all that is not utterly seductive?"

"There is no question but that we are difficult to resist . . . why, I can remember one of our judges who was the living terror of every virtue . . . but tell me, La Brie, do you really think that if I were to say a word . . ."

"It would be no sooner said than done, of that you may be sure."

"But you would have to keep a tight lip, La Brie. It is important for me not to start off my relationship with my wife by an act of infidelity."

"Oh, Monsieur, you would drive her to despair if she were to suspect; she loves you so dearly."

"Really, do you think she loves me, at least a little?"

"She adores you, Monsieur, and to be unfaithful to her would be tantamount to murder."

"And yet you think, looking at things from the opposite angle? . . ."

"That the affair will pursue its course to its inevitable conclusion, if you so desire. It all depends upon you."

"Oh, my dear La Brie, you overwhelm me. What a pleasure to be involved in two affairs, to be unfaithful to two women at the same time! To be unfaithful, my friend, unfaithful: what a delight for a man of law!"

As a result of these blandishments, Fontanis decked himself out in his finest clothing, prettified himself, forgot the lashes wherewith his bottom was lacerated, and, while keeping his wife simmering on the back burner, directed his heavy guns at the crafty Lucille who, listening to him at first with great modesty, little by little began to play his game.

This little game had been going on for about four days without anyone's seeming to notice when news sheets and gazettes were received at the château urging all astronomers to observe, on the following night, "the passage of Venus beneath the sign of Capricorn."

"Why of course!" said the judge the minute he heard the news, acting as though he were an authority. "'Tis a most singular event. I must confess I did not expect this phenomenon to occur. I have, as you may know, Mesdames, more than a nodding acquaintance with this science. I have in fact written a six-volume work on the satellites of Mars."

"On the satellites of Mars," said the marquise with a smile. "I'm surprised you chose that subject, Judge, since Mars has not been especially propitious for you."

"Always the joker, my dear Marquise. I can see that my little secret has not been kept. Be that as it may, I'm most curious to see the event of which we have just learned . . . Is there any place here, Marquis, to which we may repair to observe the trajectory of this planet?"

"Of course," the marquis replied. "Over my dovecote I have a well-equipped observatory. You will find there some excellent telescopes, quadrants, compasses, in short everything an astronomer's observation tower calls for."

"I see that you too have some knowledge of the science."

"Not in the least. But one has eyes like everyone else, and one has occasion to encounter people who are knowledgeable in astronomy and is delighted to learn from them."

"Well then, I shall be only too happy to give you a few lessons, and in six weeks I guarantee that you will have a better knowledge of the heavens than Descartes or Copernicus."

However, it was time to repair to the observatory. The judge was distressed that his wife's illness was going to deprive him of the pleasure of playing the scholar in front of her, without for one minute suspecting, poor devil, that none other than she was destined to play the principal role in this strange comedy.

Although balloons were not yet a matter of public knowledge, they were already known in 1779, and the clever physicist who was to launch the one with which we will shortly be concerned, more skillful than any of those physicists who came after him, had the good sense to show his admiration like the others and not to say a word when intruders arrived to steal his discovery away from him. In the middle of a perfectly constructed aerostat, Mademoiselle de Téroze was, according to the plan, supposed to ascend at the appointed hour clasped in the arms of Count d'Elbène, and this scene, viewed from afar and lighted only by a faint artificial light, was cleverly enough devised to fool a dolt like the judge, who had never in his life even read a single work on the science in which he prided himself.

The entire company reached the top of the tower, armed itself with telescopes, and the balloon began its ascent.

"Do you see anything?" they all asked one another.

"Not yet."

"Yes, I do."

"No, that's not it."

"I beg your pardon. Look over there, to the left. Train your telescope to the east."

"Ah! I have it, my friends," shouted the judge, going into raptures. "I have it! Follow where my telescope is pointing . . . A trifle closer to Mercury but not as far as Mars; far below the orbit of Saturn. There. Ah, Good Heavens! what a beautiful sight!"

"I have it now too," said the marquis, "and 'tis truly a marvelous sight to see. Do you see the conjunction?"

"I have it clearly in my telescope . . ."

And just as he said these words the balloon passed over the tower.

"I say," said the marquis, "is it possible that the notices we received were wrong? *For didn't we just see 'Venus over Capricorn'?*"

"You are quite right," said the judge. "That is the most beautiful spectacle I have ever seen in my life."

"Who knows," said the marquis, "whether you will always be obliged to ascend so high to see it comfortably."

"Ah! Marquis, your banter is out of place at such a beautiful moment..."

And as the balloon was by that time disappearing into darkness, they all went downstairs, highly pleased with the allegorical phenomenon that art had just lent to Nature.

"I must say I deeply regret that you did not come with us to share our pleasure at witnessing that phenomenon," said Monsieur de Fontanis to his wife, whom he found back in bed when he returned to the château. "I cannot conceive of anything more beautiful."

"I believe you," said the young woman, "but someone told me that there were all sorts of immodest things involved with this curious event, in which case I am just as happy to have missed it."

"Immodest!" said the judge with a derisive laugh that only accentuated his usual charm. "Not in the least. It was a conjunction: is there anything else in Nature? 'Tis what I should like to have happen at long last between us, and what will happen the moment you say the word. But tell me, in all good conscience, sovereign mistress of all my thought, haven't you made your slave pine long enough, and won't you soon grant him the reward for all his troubles?"

"Alas! my angel," said his young wife, her words dripping with love, "I trust you know that I am as eager as you. But you can see my condition... and you see it without feeling sorry for me, you cruel fellow, although 'tis completely your doing: if I didn't have to worry so much about things that concern you, I would feel much better."

The judge was in seventh heaven at hearing himself cajoled in this way; he strutted like a peacock, he straightened up like a ramrod: never had any man of law, not even those who had just finished a hanging, ever had a neck so stiff.

But since, in spite of all these blandishments on the part of his wife, the obstacles standing in the way of their effecting a conjunction grew greater every day, and as quite the opposite was true insofar as Lucille was concerned, Fontanis did not hesitate to choose the bird of love in the hand rather than wait for those of Hymen in the bush.

"One cannot escape me," he said to himself. "I'll always have her whenever I want her. But the other may be here for only a fleeting moment; I should lose no time taking advantage of the opportunity."

And, basing his actions on these principles, Fontanis lost no opportunity to pursue his plans.

"Alas, Monsieur," this young lady said to him one day with feigned ingenuousness, "won't I become the most unhappy of creatures if I yield and grant you what you are asking? . . . Given the ties that bind you, will you ever be able to repair the wrong that you will do my reputation?"

"What do you mean by 'repair'? One does not repair in such cases. Neither of us will have anything more to 'repair' than the other, this is what is called a wasted effort. There is never anything to fear from a married man, because his basic concern is to keep things secret,

The Mystified Magistrate ✦ 71

all of which will in no wise stop you from finding a husband."

"And what about religion, Monsieur? and honor?"

"Mere nothings, my pet. I can see that you are an artless young girl—they should have named you Agnes[17]—and that you should enroll for a few lessons in my school. Ah! I would make these childish prejudices disappear in a trice."

"But I was under the impression that your profession pledged you to respect them."

"Yes, that is true, but only for show; all we have going for us is show, we must at least make use of it to inspire respect. But once stripped of this vain decorum which compels us to show a certain respect, we resemble in every way the rest of humanity. Come now, how could you expect us to be immune to their vices? Our passions, far more heated by the recital or perpetual portrayal of theirs, make no distinction between theirs and ours save by the excesses which they fail to recognize and which constitute our daily delight. Almost always immune to the laws wherewith we make the rest of humanity tremble, we are all the more excited by this impunity, and as a consequence become even greater villains . . ."

Lucille listened to all this nonsense, and however much she may have found both the external appearance and the morality of this abominable person repulsive, she continued to offer little or no resistance to his amorous advances, for such were the terms she had agreed to as a basis for her reward. The more persistent the judge's suit became, the more his fatuousness made him unbearable. There is nothing more amusing on the face of the earth than a lawyer in love: 'tis a perfect picture of awkwardness, impertinence, and clumsiness. If the reader has ever had occasion to see a turkey in a position to multiply its species, he has an excellent idea of the picture we would like to draw from him.

Despite whatever precautions he may have taken to conceal his game, one day when his insolence made what he was up to all too obvious, the marquis could not refrain from taking him in hand and humiliating him in the presence of his goddess.

"Judge," he said to him, "I have just this minute received some most distressing news for you."

"What news?"

"We have it on good authority that the High Court of Aix is going to be eliminated. The public complains that it serve no useful purpose. Aix has far less need of a high court than does Lyon, and this last-named city, much too far removed from Paris to be dependent upon it from a judicial point of view, will be responsible for all of Provence. Lyon dominates Provence, it is positively situated as it must be to harbor within its bosom the judges of so important a province."

"Such an arrangement makes no sense whatsoever."

"It is a wise move. Aix is at the end of the world. No matter in what region a citizen of Provence may live, every last one of them would prefer to come to Lyon for his business rather than to your old mud-pit of Aix. Incredibly bad roads, no bridge over that Durance River which, like your brains, is inoperative nine months out of the year; and, what is more, shortcomings of a very special nature, I cannot pretend otherwise: first of all, they find fault with the makeup of the court; there is not, they say, a single member of the Aix court who is capable of so much as writing his own name . . . fishmongers, sailors, smugglers—in short, a whole gang of contemptible scoundrels that the nobility wants nothing to do with, an unsavory bunch that plagues and harasses the people in order to compensate for the discredit into which it has fallen . . . numbskulls, idiots . . . I beg your pardon, Judge, but I'm only passing on what people have written to me—I'll show you the letter after dinner—in a word, cads of the lowest sort, who carry their fanaticism and scandal to such lengths that they keep standing, as a proof of their integrity, an ever-ready gallows, which is nothing more than a monument to their ridiculous inflexibility. 'Tis a monument whose very foundation the people ought to destroy, in order to stone to death the notorious tormentors who, by their insolence, dare to keep this constant reminder of prison before the people's eyes. It is surprising they have not already done so, and it seems that the day may not be far off when they will[18] . . . A whole host of unjust decrees, an affectation of sternness the whole purpose of which is to cover up the legislative crimes it may please the members of the court to commit; even more serious charges; in short, and to resume all the above: unequivocal enemies of the State, not only now but from time immemorial, people are daring to say openly. The feeling of revulsion caused by your desecrations of Mérindol is still present in the people's hearts.[19] Don't you offer the most frightful spectacle it is possible in this day and age to depict? Can one imagine without shuddering the guardians of law and order, of peace and impartiality, running wild through the province like so many madmen, a torch in one hand and a knife in the other, burning, killing, raping, and massacring anything that happens their way, like a pack of maddened tigers that had escaped from the jungle? Is this any way for judges to act? One also recalls several instances when you stubbornly refused to come to the aid of the king when he needed it; you were, on more than one occasion, ready to incite the province to revolt rather than agree to the taxes assessed upon you. Do you think that this unhappy period has been forgotten when, without being threatened with any danger, you came leading the citizens of your town to bring the keys of the city to the High Constable of Bourbon who was betraying his king? Or that dark time when, trembling at the very approach of Charles V, you hastened to pay homage and to open up your gates to him? Is it not common knowledge that it was in the inner sanctum of the High Court of Aix that the first seeds of the Catholic League were sown? In short, in whatever age, that your ranks were filled with seditionists or rebels, murderers or traitors?

"You know better than anyone, ye judges of Provence, that when you are of a mind to bring about the ruination of someone, you make it your business to dig into his past, you carefully bring to light again all his former wrongdoings in order to cast an even more serious light on his present: therefore be not surprised to find others employing the same tactics with respect to you that you have used with your poor innocent victims when it pleased you to sacrifice them to your pedantry. Remember this, my dear Judge, that no individual or body of men can any longer scurrilously attack a peaceful and honest citizen, and if anybody takes it upon himself to act with such irrelevance, then one should not be surprised to see a chorus of voices raised, clamoring for the rights of the weak and for virtue as opposed to despotism and inequity."

Since the judge was unable either to answer these charges or refute them, he left the table in a blind rage, swearing that he was going to leave the house. Next to the sight of a judge in love, the second most laughable spectacle is that of a judge in a rage: his facial muscles, naturally composed by hypocrisy but suddenly obliged to move from that serene state to the contortions of rage, can only do so by violent gradations, the sight of which is comical in the extreme.

When they had been thoroughly amused at seeing the judge vent his spleen, and as they had not yet reached the stage when, if things went according to plan, they would be rid of him forever, they did their best to calm him: they followed at his heels and finally brought him back. By evening, having virtually forgotten all the little torments wherewith he had been beset that morning, Fontanis reverted to his former self, and all was forgotten.

Mademoiselle de Téroze was improving, although she outwardly still looked slightly the worse for wear. Yet she came downstairs for meals, and even joined the others for a short walk now and then. The judge, less assiduous than he had been in times past, because his thoughts were preoccupied only with Lucille, saw nonetheless that he would soon be obliged to devote all his attention to his wife. He therefore resolved to quicken the tempo of his other suit, which at that moment was at a point of crisis. Mademoiselle de Totteville had made it clear that she was ready to yield: the only problem remaining was to find a safe place of assignation. The judge suggested his bachelor quarters; Lucille, who did not sleep in the same bedroom as her parents, readily agreed, the time was set for the following evening, and without wasting a moment Lucille passed the information on to the marquis. They rehearsed her role with her, and the rest of the day was spent without incident.

About eleven o'clock, Lucille, who had been instructed by the judge to precede him into the bedchamber using a key he had given her, excused herself, telling the assembled company that she had a headache, and left the room. A quarter of an hour later, the eager judge also excused himself, but the marquise stopped him by saying that, as a special honor to him that night she wished to accompany him back to his bedchamber. All the others joined in the fun, Mademoiselle de Téroze foremost among them, and without paying the slightest heed to the judge, who was on tenterhooks and was racking his brain to try to figure out how he could escape from this ridiculous display of civility, or at least how he could forewarn the young lady whom he strongly suspected they were going to discover in his bed, they all took candles and, with the men leading the way and the bevy of ladies surrounding Fontanis—they offered him their hands—this absurd cortege slowly wended its way to his bedroom door . . .

Our ill-fated swain could scarcely breathe.

"I will not be held responsible for anything," he mumbled. "Think how rashly you are acting. How do you know that the object of my desire is not awaiting me at this very moment in my bed, and if indeed she is, have you considered all the possible ramifications that may result from your indiscretion?"

"As a precautionary measure," said the marquise,

throwing open the door, "come, ye beauty, who, we are told, awaits the judge in his bed: show thyself, be not afraid."

But imagine everyone's surprise when the lights next to the judge's bed cast their rays on an enormous jackass, which was comfortably ensconced beneath the sheets and which, by some agreeable quirk of fate, doubtless delighted by the role it was being made to play, was peacefully asleep on the judicial couch, snoring voluptuously.

"Ah! to be sure," d'Olincourt cried out, holding his sides with laughter. "My dear Judge, dwell for a moment upon how cool, calm, and collected this animal is: doesn't it remind you of one of your colleagues in the court-room?"

But the judge, pleased as punch to have wiggled out of that predicament so easily, the judge, who fancied that this practical joke would serve to cover up the rest and that Lucille, having been the first to discover it, would have done her best to take whatever steps she deemed necessary to keep their intrigue from being discovered, the judge, I say, joined in the general hilarity.

They managed to extricate as best they could the poor jackass—most distressed at having its sleep inter-rupted—the bed was outfitted with clean white sheets, and Fontanis replaced with all due dignity the most su-perb jackass the region had to offer.

"Truth to tell," said the marquise when she saw him safe and sound in bed, "it's hard to tell the difference. I would never have thought that a jackass and a judge of the High Court of Aix could look so much alike."

"That, Madame, is where you are sadly mistaken,"

replied the marquis. "Do you mean to tell me you are unaware that it is from among these learned creatures that the Court of Aix has always chosen its members? In fact, I would be willing to wager that the one we just saw leave the room was its first presiding judge."

Fontanis's first thought the following morning was to ask Lucille how she had managed so cleverly to extricate herself from the embarrassing situation. She, well rehearsed as to her answer, said that when she had realized the joke being played, she wasted no time leaving the room, but not without some concern that she had been betrayed, and this had caused her to spend a terrible night, adding that she would be on pins and needles until she was sure she had not been implicated or compromised. The judge set her mind at ease, then tried to cajole her into joining him for a return match the following night. The modest girl put up some slight show of resistance, which only made Fontanis press his suit with ever greater ardor, until at last everything was arranged in accordance with his desires.

But if their initial assignation had been interrupted by a comic scene, the second was to turn into a veritable disaster. Arrangements similar to those of the preceding night were made: Lucille was the first to retire, and the judge followed suit shortly afterward, this time without anyone interfering. He found her at the appointed tryst and, taking her in his arms, was already on the verge of offering her the unequivocal proof of his passion when the doors suddenly burst open, revealing none other than Monsieur and Madame de Totteville, the marquise, and Mademoiselle de Téroze herself.

"You monster!" she screamed, flying in a fury at her

husband, "is this the way you laugh behind my back, at my candor and tenderness!"

"Ungrateful daughter!" Monsieur de Totteville said sternly to his daughter, who had cast herself at her father's knees. "So this is how you take advantage of the freedom we have given you."

Meanwhile, the marquise and Madame de Totteville were casting exasperated glances at the guilty couple, as was Madame d'Olincourt herself, but her accusatory gaze was interrupted by her need to catch hold of her sister, who had just swooned in her arms.

It would be difficult to describe the expression on Fontanis's face as all this was going on: surprise, shame, terror, concern—all these varying emotions were vying simultaneously for the upper hand, which made him look for all the world as stiff as a statue. About this time the marquis arrived, asked what the trouble was, and when he learned what had happened was understandably indignant.

"Monsieur," said Lucille's father firmly, "I would never have expected that a girl from a fine family would have to worry about affronts of this sort in your house. I trust you will understand that I cannot under any circumstance tolerate such an insult and that I, my wife and daughter are leaving immediately to seek redress from those by whom we have been wronged."

"Really, Monsieur," the marquis d'Olincourt then said curtly to the judge, "you must admit that such scenes are hardly what I have a right to expect. Or do you mean to tell me that the only reason you sought to marry into our family was to dishonor my sister and this house?" Then, turning to Totteville: "I can only applaud your demands for redress, Monsieur, but I nonetheless most earnestly request that you make every effort to avoid a scandal. It is not for this ne'er-do-well that I ask it—he is beneath contempt and deserves only to be punished—but rather for me, Sir, for my family, and above all for my poor father-in-law who, having placed his full trust in this buffoon, will surely die of grief at having been so severely mistaken."

"I would like to oblige you, Monsieur," said Monsieur de Totteville haughtily, leading his wife and daughter away, "but you will allow me to place my honor above these considerations. You will in no wise be compromised, Monsieur, by the complaints I intend to lodge; the only person implicated will be this dishonest fellow"—pointing to Fontanis—"and now, if you will allow me, I have heard enough and must be off forthwith, for vengeance calls."

With these words, the three of them strode from the room with such purpose that nothing in the world could have stopped them; they were, so the assembled throng was assured, off to Paris as fast as they could go to present a petition to the court demanding redress for the outrages that Judge Fontanis would surely have committed had he not been stopped in the nick of time.

Meanwhile, back at the château, all was a scene of desolation and despair. Mademoiselle de Téroze, so recently recovered, had taken to her bed again with a fever which, everyone was told, was dangerously high. Monsieur and Madame d'Olincourt were raining insult after insult upon the judge, who, since he had no other sanctuary than this house, given the untenable situation in which he found himself, did not dare respond to the reprimands that were so deservingly addressed to him. Things remained at this pass for three days, when secret information reached the marquis informing him at last that the matter was considered to be of the utmost gravity, that it was being dealt with as a criminal case, and that the court was about to issue a warrant for Fontanis's arrest.

"What! Without hearing *my* side of the story?" said the terrified judge.

"Isn't that the rule?" d'Olincourt replied. "Does the court allow the person for whom a warrant has been issued any means of defense? Isn't it one of your most cherished customs to sully a defendant's good name before you hear him out? They are only using against you the same weapons you have used against so many others. After serving for thirty years the cause of injustice, doesn't it seem reasonable that you should become, at least once in your life, its victim?"

"But all that fuss because of a girl?"

"What do you mean, because of a girl? Don't you know that these are the most dangerous cases? Was that wretched affair, the very memory of which cost you no less than five hundred lashes in the haunted château, anything else but over some girls? And, if memory serves, didn't you judge that a matter involving some girls was sufficient cause for you to sully a gentleman's honor? Hammurabi's law, Judge, an eye for an eye: 'tis the compass you steer by; therefore submit to it bravely."

"Good Heavens!" said Fontanis. "In the name of God, my dear brother, do not abandon me."

"You may count on us to stand by you," d'Olincourt replied. "No matter how you may have dishonored us, no matter what cause for complaint we may have against you, you can indeed count on us. But the means are not easy . . . you know what they are."

"What are they?"

"The king's favor. A *lettre de cachet*.[20] That's the only possibility I see."

"What a terrible plight!"

"I agree. But what are your other choices? Would you prefer to leave France and be ruined forever, when a few years of prison may well atone for the entire affair? Besides, haven't you and your fellow judges sometimes resorted to this same means? Wasn't it by such barbaric advice that you succeeded in finally crushing that nobleman whom the ghosts avenged so well? Didn't you have the gall—by means of a bold lie as dangerous as it is punishable—to place this poor officer between the Scylla of prison and the Charybdis of disgrace, and to cease your contemptible thunderbolts only upon condition that he would be crushed by those of his king? Consequently, my friend, there is nothing surprising about what I suggest to you: not only is this path one you yourself have traveled, but it is now one you ought to welcome."

"O dreadful memories!" said the judge, tears streaming down his cheeks. "Who would have believed that Heaven's revenge would fall upon me almost at the very moment when my crimes were being committed! What I have done is being paid back. All I can do is suffer, suffer in silence."

Nevertheless, as some help was most urgently required, the marquise urgently advised her husband to leave for Fontainebleau, where the court was then in residence. Mademoiselle de Téroze took no part in this family council: shame and grief without, and Count d'Elbène within, kept her constantly confined to her bed-chamber, the door of which was locked to the judge. He had come and knocked on her door on several occasions, and tried by tears and a display of remorse to persuade her to open it, but always to no avail.

So the marquis departed. The journey was not long, and two days later he was back, escorted by two officers and bearing with him an alleged order the very sight of which caused the judge to tremble from head to foot.

"Your timing couldn't be better," said the marquise, who pretended that she had received news from Paris while her husband was away at the court. "The case is proceeding with incredible speed, and my friends have written me urging me to help the judge escape without a moment's delay. My father has been informed of the matter; he is in a state of despair difficult to describe. He enjoins us to serve his friend faithfully, and to depict to him the suffering which this whole matter has caused him . . . His health, alas, does not allow him to offer any more substantial help than his best wishes, which would have been more sincere had his friend been a whit less foolish . . . Here is the letter."

The marquis gave it a cursory glance, and after having lectured Fontanis, who was having a hard time reconciling himself to the thought of going to prison, he turned him over to the guards, who were none other than two sergeants from his own regiment, and urged Fontanis to be comforted by the fact that he fully intended to keep in constant contact with him.

"I have," the marquis said to him, "managed with great difficulty to obtain a fortified château six or seven leagues from here. There you will be under the command of one of my old friends, who will treat you as though you were me. I am sending a personal message with these guards reiterating in the strongest language my requests about how deferential they should be with you. Therefore, go with your mind at rest."

The judge blubbered like a baby: nothing is as bitter as a conscience-stricken criminal who sees himself beset with all the scourges that he himself has earlier employed . . . but, nonetheless, there was no delaying the departure any longer. The judge made one final urgent request: permission to kiss his wife good-bye.

"Your wife!" the marquise said to him brusquely. "She is, I am happy to say, not yet that; and in the midst of all our misfortunes, that is our only consolation."

"So be it," said the judge. "I shall somehow find the courage to bear this further wound." And so saying he climbed into the carriage manned by his guards.

The château to which this poor wretch was being taken was part of Madame d'Olincourt's dowry, and there all was in readiness to receive him. A captain of d'Olincourt's regiment, a harsh and forbidding man, was picked to play the role of the commanding officer of the prison. He received Fontanis, dismissed the guards, and said harshly to his prisoner as he assigned him to the barest of rooms, that he had received further orders concerning him that were so strict he had no choice but to follow them to the letter.

The judge was left in this cruel situation for almost a month. Not a single visitor came to see him; he was fed only soup, bread, and water; for a bed, he had only some loose straw, and his room was frightfully humid. The only time anyone came to see him was—as is the custom in the Bastille; that is, the way they treat animals in the zoo—to bring him food. During the period of this fateful incarceration, the poor lawyer had ample time for bitter reflections, which no one interrupted. At length the pseudo-commander appeared and, after offering him a few meager words of consolation, spoke to him in the following manner:

"You should have realized, Monsieur," he said, "that your initial mistake was to have wished to marry into a family so far above you in every respect. Baron de Téroze and Marquis d'Olincourt are gentlemen of the highest nobility, the fairest flowers of all France, and you are but a poor lawyer from Provence, without station or name, without fame or fortune. If only you had taken the time or trouble to give the matter a little serious thought, you would doubtless have realized that it was your bounden duty to inform the Baron de Téroze, who willfully blinded himself to the truth about you, namely that you were no worthy match for his daughter. Moreover, how could you for a moment have imagined that this girl, who is as lovely as love itself, could ever become the wife of a filthy old monkey like yourself? One has a right to be blind to one's faults, but not to that extent!

"The reflections you must have made during your stay here, Monsieur, have surely convinced you that during the four months you spent at the Marquis d'Olincourt's you were a laughingstock for everyone, no more. Persons of your station and appearance, your profession and stupidity, your spitefulness and double-dealing, ought to expect nothing but this kind of treatment. By a thousand tricks, one more clever or amusing than the next, they kept you from enjoying the young lady to whom you aspired. They gave you five hundred lashes in a haunted château; they showed you your wife in the arms of the man she adores—which you in your stupidity mistook for a celestial phenomenon; they succeeded in getting you amorously involved with a well-paid whore, who made a complete fool out of you. And, finally, they locked you up in this château, where the Marquis d'Olincourt, the colonel of my regiment, can keep you for the rest of your days—which he will most certainly do if you refuse to sign the paper I have in my hand. May I point out, Sir, before you read it, that as far as the world at large is concerned," the pseudo-commander went on, "you are merely the man who is a suitor for the hand of Mademoiselle de Téroze, and not her husband. Your marriage took place in the strictest intimacy; what few witnesses there were have agreed to swear they know nothing about it. The priest who performed the ceremony has given back the marriage certificate, which I have here. The notary has likewise returned the marriage contract, which you see before your very eyes. What is more, you have never slept with your wife: your marriage is therefore invalid and is tacitly annulled, with the full consent of all parties, which gives the breach as much validity as though it were sanctioned by the religious and civil laws. What is more, I have here the baron's statement of withdrawal, as well as his daughter's. All we need now is yours. The choice is yours, Monsieur: the amicable signature of this document, or the certainty that you will end your days here . . . That is all I have to say. The floor is yours."

After a moment's reflection, the judge took the document and read these words:

> I declare and affirm, to whomsoever it may concern,
> that I have never been Mademoiselle de Téroze's hus-
> band. By the present document I render unto her all
> the rights which for a certain period of time were
> thought to have been given to me with respect to her,
> and I further swear that I shall never reclaim them so
> long as I shall live. Furthermore, I have only the high-
> est praise for the many kindnesses and considerations
> bestowed upon me by her and her family during the
> summer I have spent in their house. It is by common
> consent and with mutual good will that we both re-
> nounce any plans for marriage that may have existed
> between us and render each unto the other the free-
> dom to dispose of our persons as though there had
> never been any intention of joining us together.
>
> I further declare that I sign the present document
> of my own volition, and in a state of reason and good
> health.
>
> Done at the Château de Valnord, belonging to
> Madame la Marquise d'Olincourt.

"You have informed me, Monsieur," said the judge
after he had read the above, "what fate I might expect if
I refused to sign, but you have failed to tell me what
might happen to me if I were to consent to everything."

"Your reward will be your immediate release, Monsieur," the pseudo-commander resumed, "and this jewel,
worth two hundred *louis*, which Madame la Marquise
d'Olincourt most earnestly begs you to accept. Plus the
assurance that you will find your valet awaiting you at the
château gate, together with two stout horses ready to
carry you back to Aix."

"I shall sign and depart, Monsieur. I am too bent upon ridding myself of all these people for me to hesitate for even a moment."

"I am most happy to hear it, Judge," said the captain, taking the signed document from him and handing him the jewel in return, "but be careful how you act in the future. Once outside, if you should ever be tempted by an obsessive desire for revenge, bear in mind, before you try anything, that you would be dealing with a formidable adversary, that this powerful family to whom you would be giving offense in its entirety by your suit, would immediately have you taken for a madman, and you would spend the rest of your days in one of those wretched insane asylums."

"Have no fear, Monsieur. No one is more interested than I in avoiding any further contact with such persons, and I can assure you I shall take every precaution to do so."

"I strongly suggest you do, Judge," said the captain, finally unlocking his prison door. "Go in peace, and may this region of France never set eyes on you again."

"You have my solemn word," said the lawyer, climbing onto his horse. "This little adventure has cured me of all my vices. If I were to live for another thousand years, I should never come to Paris looking for a wife. I have upon occasion had some inkling of how it felt to be cuckolded after one was married, but I had never suspected that it was possible to wear the horns before . . . I can further say that my judicial decisions will henceforth be governed by wisdom and discretion. No longer shall I set myself up as mediator between whores and men more worthy than I: the cost is too high to side with these ladies of easy virtue, and I want nothing more to do with people whose minds and hearts are intent upon revenge."

With these words the judge departed and, having grown wise at his own expense, was never heard from again. The whores complained that they no longer received any judicial support in Provence, and as a result virtue flowered in that region because the young girls, seeing that they could no longer count on this prop, preferred the path of virtue to the dangers that might await them on the road of vice whenever the magistrates became wise enough to realize the terrible disadvantages of supporting them through their protection.

The reader may well imagine that during the time of the judge's incarceration, the Marquis d'Olincourt, after having made the baron change his mind about his overly favorable impression of Fontanis, had bent his every effort to making sure that all the arrangements of which we have just read were faithfully carried out. Thanks to his skill and influence, he succeeded so well in this endeavor that three months later Mademoiselle de Téroze was married, in a public ceremony, to Count d'Elbène, with whom she lived in perfect bliss.

"There are times when I have some pangs of regret at having mistreated this scurvy fellow," the marquis said one day to his dear sister-in-law. "But when I see on the one hand the happiness that has resulted from my efforts, and when on the other I realize more and more that the person I persecuted was nothing but a socially useless clown, essentially an enemy of the State, a person given to disturbing the public peace, one who set himself up as the tormentor of a decent and respectable family and slandered a distinguished nobleman whom I respect and to whose family I have the honor of belonging, I find consolation and echo the words of the well-known philosopher: 'O sovereign Providence, why is it the ways of man are so restricted that they can never manage to do good save by a touch of evil.'"*

---

*This tale was finished on July 16, 1787, at ten o'clock in the evening.

EMILIE DE TOURVILLE
or
FRATERNAL CRUELTY

Nothing is more sacred than a family's honor, but if this treasure, no matter how precious, in any way becomes tarnished, should those in whose interest it is to defend it go so far as to assume the humiliating mantle of persecuting those poor creatures who, it has been assumed, have sullied them? Would it not be reasonable to assume that the unspeakable acts with which they have tormented their victim more than compensate for the wrong—often imagined—they feel has been done them? Who ultimately is the more guilty in the eyes of reason, a weak young lady who has been betrayed or a family relative who, claiming to take revenge in order to cleanse the blot on one's escutcheon, becomes the torturer of that poor creature? The story we are about to relate may perhaps shed some light on that question.

The Count de Luxeuil, who bore the title of lieutenant-general in His Majesty's service,[1] a man of fifty-six or fifty-seven, on his way home by post chaise from one of his properties in Picardy, was passing through the Compiègne Forest about six o'clock one

November evening when he heard a woman's cry, seemingly emanating from one of the roads parallel to the
main thoroughfare along which he was traveling. He
stopped and ordered his valet, who was trotting along beside the post chaise, to go and see what it was. The valet
returned shortly to report that the source of the cries was
a young woman of about sixteen or seventeen, so covered in her own blood that it was impossible to tell where
the bleeding was coming from, who was calling for help.
The count immediately descended from his carriage and
flew in the direction of the poor creature; he too, partly
because of the increasing darkness, had trouble telling
where the blood she was losing was coming from, though
it looked as if it was from the veins in her arms, where
normally doctors were wont to bleed a patient.

"Mademoiselle," said the count, after trying to ad-
minister whatever help he could on the spot, "this is neither the time nor place to ask you what has brought you
to this pass, nor clearly are you in any state to tell me.
Please, come with me to my carriage and be assured that
my sole concern now is to calm you down and to render
you whatever help I can."

Saying which, the count and his valet carried the
poor girl to the carriage, and off they went.

Scarcely had this intriguing young lady realized that
she was no longer in danger than she tried to stammer
some words of gratitude, but the count begged her not
even to try.

"Mademoiselle," he said, "tomorrow you can tell
me, I hope, just what has befallen you, but today, by the
authority vested in me by age and by my good fortune of

being in a position to help you, I most urgently ask that you simply try to regain your composure."

They arrived; in order to avoid attracting any undue attention, the count wrapped his charge in a man's cloak and had his valet escort the young lady to a convenient apartment at the far end of the house. As soon as he had exchanged embraces with his wife and son, who were awaiting him for dinner, he made his excuses and hurried off to see her. He took the local surgeon with him, who examined the young woman: she was in an indescribable state of physical prostration and seeming depression, and of a pallor that made one think that she had but a few moments left to live, and yet there was no visible wound the doctor could detect. Her weakness, she told them, stemmed from the enormous amount of blood she had lost for the past three months, and as she was on the point of telling the count the unnatural reason for that prodigious loss, she fainted, and the surgeon urged she be allowed to rest and that, for the moment, he recommended giving her only some calmatives and cordials.

Our poor young woman spent a relatively peaceful night, but for the next six days was still in no condition to tell her benefactor the events leading up to his discovering her in the forest that night. Finally, on the evening of the seventh day—no one in the count's house still had any inkling the young lady was there, and she, because of the precautions taken to keep her presence a secret, had no idea under whose roof she was lodged—she begged the count to hear her out, and above all to show her forbearance, no matter how grievous the faults to which she might confess.

The count pulled up a chair, assuring his protégée that she had already piqued his interest beyond compare, and that she need not fear, he was all ears. So it was our beautiful adventuress began the story of her misfortunes.

MADEMOISELLE
DE TOURVILLE'S STORY

I, Sir, am the daughter of the Presiding Judge de Tourville, who is too well known and too distinguished in his profession for me tell you further about him. It has been two years since I left the convent, and during my first few months home I did not set foot from my father's house. Having lost my mother when I was still very young, he alone assumed the task of taking care of my education, and I can say that he went to great lengths to give me all the graces and amenities of my sex. This attentiveness on his part, plus his stated intention to see that I was as well married as it was in his power to arrange, and, I must say, a touch of favoritism toward me, all this, I say, soon awakened in both my brothers a certain degree of jealousy. My oldest brother, who had just turned twenty-six, had already been named a judge of the provincial court three years before, and my other brother, who would soon be twenty-four, has recently been named a legal counselor.

I had no idea that they hated me as strongly as I now know they did. Having done nothing to deserve those feelings on their part, I lived under the illusion that they were as fond of me as I was, in my sweet innocence, of them. O just heaven! How wrong I was. Except for the

time taken up by my studies, I enjoyed the greatest freedom in my father's house; he imposed no restrictions
upon me, and for the last eighteen months I had his permission to go out for daily walks in the company of my
maid. We either walked along the terrace of the Tuileries
gardens or along the ramparts not far from where we
lived. Or, upon occasion, always with my maid, we would
either walk—or sometimes take my father's carriage—
and pay a visit to relatives or friends, though we would
never make these visits at times when it would be im-
proper for a young lady to be alone at such gatherings. All
my misfortunes emanate from this accursed freedom,
which is why I mention it to you, Sir. Would to God that I
had never been granted that freedom!

About a year ago, I was out walking, as I have mentioned to you, with my maid, whose name is Julie, along
a rather dimly lit path in the Tuileries, where I thought it
would be less crowded than on the terrace and where I
felt the air would be more bracing. Suddenly, from out of
nowhere, six rowdy young men accosted us and made it
clear from the foul language they used that they took us
both to be women of little virtue, if that is the term. Horribly embarrassed by such a scene, and not knowing how
to extricate myself from it, I was about to seek safety in
flight when a young man whom I had frequently seen
out alone taking walks more or less at the same time as
ours, and who looked like a proper gentleman, happened
by in the thick of this frightful scene.

"Monsieur!" I cried out to him. "You don't have the
honor of knowing me, but we have crossed paths almost
every day in the course of our walks. What you have seen
of me, I trust, must have convinced you that I am not an

adventuress. I beg you most urgently to give me your hand and escort me home, away from the clutches of these ruffians."

Monsieur de *** (I shall if you please not divulge his name, for all sorts of good and valid reasons) hurried over, scattered the young rapscallions to the four winds, convincing them by the polite and respectful manner in which he greeted me that they had made an egregious error. Upon which he took my arm and led me from the garden.

"Mademoiselle," he said as we approached the door to my house, "I think it would be wise if I took my leave here. If I escort you to your door, you might be obliged to explain my presence, as a result of which you might be forbidden to take any further walks unescorted. So don't tell a soul what just happened and do keep coming, as you have in the past, to that same path, since you seem to enjoy it and your parents allow it. As for me, I shall be there every day without fail, and you should know that if anyone ever tries to accost or in any way disturb you, I stand ready to lay down my life in your defense."

Such a declaration and tempting offer made me look at this young man with somewhat different eyes than I had till then. He was quite handsome, and I judged him to be roughly two or three years older than I. As I thanked him, I found myself blushing, and before I had time to ward them off, the ardent features of this seductive god, who today is the source of all my afflictions, had already pierced my heart. We separated, but I had the clear impression by the way he took his leave that I had made the same impression on him as he had made on me.

I went back to my father's house and carefully refrained from mentioning anything that had happened. The next day I returned to that same pathway, spurred on by some uncontrollable feeling, one that would have made me brave any danger I might have encountered there . . . What am I saying, I would rather have willed them to happen so that this same gallant person might perhaps once again come to my rescue. I am doubtless portraying my feelings too naively to you, Sir, but you have promised to bear with me and hear me out, and each new facet of my story will show you that I am right to ask for your forbearance: that is not the only imprudent act I committed, nor will it be the only time I shall stand in need of your compassion.

Monsieur de *** appeared on the pathway six minutes after I arrived, and as soon as he saw me he came up to me and said:

"Dare I ask, Mademoiselle, whether there have been any negative repercussions from yesterday's incident and whether you have suffered any ill effects as a result of it?"

I assured him everything was fine on both counts, saying that I had indeed followed his advice, and thanked him once again for his help. Nothing, I now felt certain, would stand in the way of my pleasure at taking these bracing morning walks.

"If you derive a certain pleasure from coming here, Mademoiselle," Monsieur de *** went on in the most civil of tones, "those who have the pleasure of meeting you in this place doubtless derive even more, and if I was so bold as to offer you that advice yesterday to say nothing that might interfere with your daily walks, the truth is you have no reason to be grateful to me, for I was working more for myself than for you." And as he spoke those words, the expression in his eyes as he gazed into mine . . . Oh, Monsieur, is it possible that such a decent, gentle man could one day be the source of all my misfortunes?

I answered him with complete candor, and we struck up a conversation as we took two full turns around the garden. Monsieur de *** refused to let me leave before I told him who it was he had had the honor of helping the previous day. I saw no reason not to give him my name, and he in turn introduced himself, after which we went our separate ways.

For almost a month, Monsieur, we saw each other in this manner every single day, and as you can well imagine, before the month was out we had confessed to each other our true feelings, without going so far, however, as to swear to our undying love.

Ultimately, Monsieur de *** beseeched me to let him see me someplace less crowded than a public garden.

"I don't dare call on you at your father's, dear Emilie," he said to me, "since I've never had the honor of being properly introduced to him, and he might well suspect the motives of my visit. Such a step, rather than helping further our plans, might do just the opposite. But if you are really kind and caring enough not to let me die of a broken heart by refusing to grant me what I dare ask of you, then I shall tell you how it can be arranged."

At first I turned a deaf ear to any such proposal, but I soon weakened and asked him just what he had in mind. What he proposed, Sir, was that we meet three times a week at the house of one Madame Berceil, a milliner whose shop was on the rue des Arcis.[2] He added that he could vouch for the woman's discretion and honesty, which he said were on a par with those of his own mother.

"Since your father gives you permission to visit your aunt, who you have told me lives not far from Madame Berceil, you need only announce that you are going to pay her a visit, which indeed you shall for a short time, then spend the rest of the time that you would have spent with your aunt at Madame Berceil's. If anyone ever inquires of your aunt whether you had indeed come to see her on the day you had announced you would, she will respond in the affirmative. Therefore, it is only a matter of timing the length of your visits carefully, and you may be sure that so long as you are trusted no one will ever think to query her on that score."

I shall spare you, Sir, the details of the many objections I raised to his proposal, to convince him how unwise it was and all the dangers it posed. What would be the point of listing for you those objections, since in the end I did succumb? I promised Monsieur de *** whatever he wanted, and the twenty *louis* he slipped to Julie without my knowledge won her over completely to his cause, while I for my part was working assiduously to seal my own doom. To seal it even more securely, as well as to intoxicate myself even longer and at greater leisure with the sweet poison that was seeping into my heart, I told my aunt an out-and-out lie: I informed her that one of my young friends (a woman I had sworn to secrecy and who had promised to respond to anyone's questions with appropriate reassurances), had been good enough to invite me to join her three times a week in her box at the National Theatre. I didn't dare tell my father, I told her, for fear he might raise some objection, but what I would tell him is that I was visiting my aunt on those days, and I begged her to swear that what I said was true. She hesitated at first, but finally yielded to my pleas, and what we arranged was that Julie would come to see her in my place and that after the play I would stop by, pick her up, and go home together. I showered my aunt with grateful kisses. Oh, how passion can blind one completely! I was thanking her for helping contribute to my downfall, for helping me open the door to the transgressions that were about to bring me to the very edge of the grave!

And so at long last our meetings at Madame Berceil's house began. Her store was impeccable, her house completely respectable. She was a woman of forty or so, in whom I thought I could confide without reservation. Alas, I placed far too much trust not only in her but also in my lover . . . perfidious man that he turned out to be. For it is time to confess, Monsieur, that in the course of my sixth visit to that accursed house, he had acquired such a hold over me, and was so totally seductive, that I became in his arms the idol of his passion and the victim of my own . . . Cruel pleasures, how many tears have you caused me to shed? With how much remorse have you broken my heart, and how much more is yet to come, till I draw my final breath?

A full year passed in this deadly illusion, Monsieur. I had just turned seventeen. Day after day my father spoke of finding me a proper husband, which made me shudder at the very prospect, when a fateful event finally occurred that hurled me into the eternal abyss into which I was plunged. It was doubtless with the sad permission of Providence that something of which I was completely innocent served to punish the sins of which I was indeed guilty, in order to show that we never escape from her clutches, that she follows whomsoever strays from the straight and narrow, and that it is from the event that one least suspects she fashions, little by little, her instrument of revenge.

Monsieur de *** had informed me one day that some indispensable business matter was going to detain him and prevent him from enjoying the pleasure of the full three hours of my company that we were wont to spend together. Still, he assured me, he would arrive for the last minutes of our allotted time, suggesting that, so as not to alter our normal procedure, I should nonetheless come at the usual time to Madame Berceil's. Spending an hour or two with her and her shop girls, he reminded me, would still be more fun than if I were to spend that same time by myself at home. I had sufficient confidence in the good lady not to raise any objection to my lover's proposal, so I promised to do as he said, only begging him not to keep me waiting too long. He assured me he would wind up his business with all due speed, and I arrived at Madame Berceil's. O what a terrible day it would turn out to be for me!

Madame Berceil greeted me at the entrance of her shop, but did not allow me to go upstairs as was our custom.

"Mademoiselle," she said as soon as she saw me, "I'm actually delighted that Monsieur de *** cannot make it today at the appointed hour. I have something I must tell you in utter confidence, something I daren't tell him. It requires both of us to leave these premises for a brief moment, which we couldn't do if he were here."

"But what exactly are you referring to?" I asked, a bit taken aback by her words of greeting.

"Nothing serious, Mademoiselle, a mere trifle," she went on. "Do set your mind at rest, it's a matter of no importance. My mother has become aware of your affair with Monsieur de ***. She's an old shrew, as straitlaced as any priest of the Church. I indulge her because she has money. Anyway, she's made it very clear she doesn't want you to meet here anymore, which somehow I couldn't bring myself to tell Monsieur de ***. In any case, here's what I thought we might do. I'm going to take you straightaway to a lady friend of mine, a woman my own age and fully as discreet. I'll introduce you, and if you like her you'll inform Monsieur de *** that I've taken you there, that this woman is decent and honorable and you're perfectly comfortable with the notion that your meetings will henceforth take place at her house. If she doesn't make a good impression on you, which I seriously doubt, then there's no point in even mentioning it to him, since we'll only have stayed there for a few moments. In which case, I'll take it upon myself to inform him that I can no longer lend him my premises, and you two can work it out together where you should meet in the future."

Madame Berceil's words were so straightforward, her manner and tone so natural, my trust in her so complete and my innocence so unequivocal, that I hadn't the slightest problem agreeing to her proposal. My only regret was that it would be henceforth impossible, for the reasons she had explained, for us to enjoy her hospitality. I thanked her for all her generosity to date, and together we left the house. The place to which she took me was on the same street as hers, only sixty or eighty steps away. From the outside, the house looked completely respectable: a coach door, lovely casement window looking onto the street: the whole place exuded an air of decency and propriety. And yet a secret voice deep within my heart seemed to cry out to me that some untoward event would befall me in that ill-fated house. With every step I took up the stairs I felt an increasing repugnance; everything seemed to be saying to me: "Where are you going, you poor girl? Run, run away as fast as you can from this abominable place . . ."

We reached the top of the stairs and entered a rather handsome antechamber, which was empty, and from there proceeded into a drawing room, the door to which immediately closed, as if someone had been lurking behind it. I began to shake like a leaf. The room was dark, so dark in fact it was hard to make one's way through it. Barely had we taken three or four steps than I felt myself seized from behind by two women, at which point the door to a small side room opened, revealing a man about fifty years old flanked by two other women.

"Off with her clothes," these two woman shouted at the two who had grabbed me, "take off all her clothes and don't bring her over here till she is stark naked."

When the first two women had taken me by surprise it was as if I had lost my wits. Regaining them, I realized that my possible salvation lay not in giving in to fright but in raising my voice as loud and long as possible. My shouts would have awakened the dead, and Madame Berceil did her best to calm me down.

"This will take but a minute, Mademoiselle," she said. "Just relax, I beg of you, and I'll be fifty *louis* the richer for it."

"You horrible creature!" I shouted, "don't think for a moment that my honor is for sale. If you don't let me go this minute, I swear I'll jump out the window!"

"Silly child," responded one of the female scoundrels, "if you did you'd only land in the courtyard of this house and you'd be quickly recaptured." Saying which she ripped off my clothes, adding: "If you want my advice, the quickest way for you to leave here is to relax and let happen what will."

Oh, Monsieur, spare me the rest of the frightful details. I was stripped naked in a trice, my shouts were stifled by methods I can only say were barbaric, and I was dragged toward this vile man who made sport of my tears and obviously was enjoying my efforts to wrest free, giving his full attention to making use of this miserable victim whose heart he was breaking. The two women continued to keep a tight grip on me and deliver me over to this monster, who, having me completely in his power, could do with me what he would. And yet he doused the fires of his guilty ardor with but some impure probing and equally odious kisses, which nonetheless left my honor intact . . .

They quickly helped me on with my clothes and turned me back over to Madame Berceil. Barely conscious, my mind clouded and bewildered, filled with a kind of dark and bitter anger that froze the tears deep within my heart, I looked at that women with uncontrolled fury.

"Mademoiselle," she began even before we had left the antechamber, and even in my state of rage I could see that she was terribly upset, "I sense the full horror of what I have just done, but I beg you to forgive me . . . as well as think long and hard before you contemplate creating a scandal. If you tell Monsieur de *** what has happened, there is no point in trying to convince him that you were brought here against your will. The 'sin' of which you are guilty is one he will never forgive, and to inform him of it will mean the end of your relationship with the man you most want to spare, since you no longer have any way of restoring the honor which he has taken from you except by his agreeing to marry you. And you may be sure that if you tell him what happened today he will never consent to ask for your hand."

"You vile woman," I said, "why have you plunged me into this abyss, why have you placed me in such a situation where my choices are either to deceive my lover or lose both my honor and him?"

"Not so fast, young lady. Let's not waste any more time talking about what is done. We haven't much time: let's focus on what *needs* to be done. If you speak out you are lost. If on the other hand you don't say a word, then my house will always be open to you, no one will ever betray you, and you will keep your lover. Think about it: if you decide to take revenge on me—and I couldn't give a fig if you decided to, since I hold the key to your little secret and will always have Monsieur de *** to fall back on—if, I say, you think it will give you some little pleasure to try to avenge yourself, dwell for a moment on all the frightful repercussions that would result . . ."

Realizing fully at that point what a terrible woman I was dealing with, and overwhelmed by the force of her reasonings, however frightful they were, I said:

"Let us leave this house, Madame, I don't want to linger here another instant. I shall say nothing of all this, as will you. I shall continue to use your services, since I cannot break off our relations without the most dire consequences, which I most eagerly desire not be revealed. But know full well that in my heart of hearts I hate and despise you as thoroughly as you deserve to be."

We made our way back to Madame de Berceil's. Good Lord! As if I had not had my share of trouble for one day, I was greeted by the news that Monsieur de *** had already been there, that he had been told that Madame was out on some urgent business and that Mademoiselle had not yet arrived. At the same time, one of the shop girls handed me a note that he had hastily penned for me. All it said was: "I did not find you here. I imagine that you were detained from coming at the usual hour. I cannot see you today, since I cannot wait. I'll see you two days hence, without fail."

I was not reassured by the note, the cold tone of which did not seem to augur well. Couldn't wait, so little patience . . . All that upset me more than I can describe. Was it possible he knew all about what had happened, that he had followed us? In which case was I not lost, a poor dishonored creature? Berceil was just as worried as I, and checking with her shop girls she learned that Monsieur de *** had arrived no more than three minutes after we had left the premises, that he had seemed quite upset, and that he had left but come back perhaps half an hour later to scribble the note. More upset than ever, I sent someone to fetch me a carriage. But would you believe, Monsieur, the impudence of that woman Berceil, the degree to which she was steeped in vice?

"Mademoiselle," she said to me, seeing I was about to leave, "remember, your lips are sealed. I trust a word to the wise is sufficient. But if you and Monsieur de *** should ever break off relations, believe me, you ought to think about taking advantage of your newfound freedom and participate in these little pleasure parties. Far better than having a single lover. I know, I know you're a proper lady and all that, but you are young, and I'm sure your family doesn't give you much spending money. You're such a pretty young thing, I could help you make as much money as you like . . . Come, come now, you're not the only one. There are endless numbers of fine ladies, many from the best families, who end up marrying marquises and counts, who either of their own accord or through the intermediary of their governesses, have passed through our hands as you have today. We have special customers who are ready and waiting for little dolls like you, as you have seen for yourself.[3] These gentlemen use them as they would a rose: they enjoy the fragrance but make sure the flower itself is not withered. Farewell, my pet, and in any event let there be no bad blood between us. As you can see, I may yet be useful to you."

I cast a look of horror upon this vile creature and quickly left without responding. I picked Julie up at my aunt's as was my custom, and returned home.

I had no way of contacting Monsieur de ***. Since we saw each other three times a week we were not in the habit of writing. Thus I would have to wait until our next assignation . . . What was he going to say to me? . . . What would I answer? Should I keep the whole thing a secret? Wasn't there a danger in that, namely that it might come to light anyway? Wouldn't it therefore be wiser to make a full confession? . . . All these different possibilities kept me in a state of indescribable anxiety. Finally I made up my mind to follow Berceil's advice. It was in her self-interest to keep the secret, and so I decided to follow her lead and keep my own lips sealed as well. Good heavens! What was the point of endlessly mulling all these possible courses of action, since I was never to see my lover again and because the lightning bolt that was about to strike me was already flashing its warning signs on all sides.

The day following that frightful incident, my eldest brother asked me why it was I took it upon myself to leave the house so many days each week and at such odd hours.

"I spend the afternoons with our aunt," I replied.

"That's not true, Emilie," he said. "You haven't set foot there in a month."

Trembling now, I said to him: "The fact is, my dear brother, that one of my lady friends—you know her, Madame de St. Clair—has been kind enough to invite me to join her three times a week in her box at the National Theatre. I didn't dare tell Father about it for fear he would disapprove. But Auntie knows all about it."

"Ah, so you're going to the theatre," my brother said. "You should have told me, I would have been happy to escort you there and bring you home. That would have been so much simpler. But to go there alone, with someone to whom you're not even related and who is almost as young as you . . ."

"Come, come now, my friend," said my other brother, who had come into the room while we were talking, "Mademoiselle has her little pleasures, and far be it for us to interfere with them . . . She's doubtless out looking for a husband, and with that kind of behavior chances are she is honey to all those buzzing bees . . ."

And with that they both turned and left the room without further word. I have to confess that their conversation frightened me no end. And yet my eldest brother seemed convinced by my story about going to the theatre, and I felt that I had sufficiently pulled the wool over his eyes that he would let matters lie. Be that as it may, even if they had carried things further, short of locking me up in my room, nothing could have prevented me from keeping our next rendezvous. It had become absolutely essential for me to clear the air with Monsieur de ***, and neither all the king's horses nor all the king's men could have kept me from going.

As for my father, nothing had changed: he still worshiped the ground I walked on, had not the slightest inkling of my misdeeds, and did nothing to restrict the freedom he had granted me. How cruel it is to deceive such good and decent parents, and how deep the remorse that emanates from such deceit, strewing thorns upon the pleasures one buys at the expense of this kind of betrayal. May this example of how cruel passion can too easily lead us to disaster teach those who may find themselves in a similar situation from making the same mistake, and may the suffering I have known, as punishment for my criminal pleasures, keep them from venturing beyond the edge of the precipice, if ever they hear of my terrible tale.

The fatal day finally dawned. With Julie beside me, I slipped out of the house as usual. Dropping her off at my aunt's, I quickly made my way by cab to Berceil's house. Stepping down from the cab, I found the house couched in darkness and strangely silent, which at first alarmed me greatly. Not a familiar face anywhere; the only person there was an elderly lady whom I had never set eyes on before and who, to my great misfortune, I was to see in the future all too often. She told me to remain in the room where I was and that Monsieur de ***, whom she named, would be with me shortly. I was overwhelmed by a feeling of utter cold, and collapsed into a chair without having the strength to respond. Scarcely was I seated when both my brothers appeared out of nowhere, pistol in hand.

"You wretched creature," my eldest brother shouted, "so this is how you lie to us! If you put up the slightest resistance, if you utter so much as one word, you're as good as dead. Come with us, we're about to teach you what happens to those who betray both their family, which you have dishonored, and the lover to whom they have given themselves."

As he spoke these last words, I lost consciousness, and when I came to I found myself in the back of a carriage, which appeared to be traveling at a very fast pace. In the carriage with me were my two brothers and the old woman I have already mentioned. My legs were tied, and both my hands tightly bound with a handkerchief.

My tears, which till that point I had held in check by the depth of my despair, now started to flow freely and for an hour I was in such a state that, no matter how guilty I may have been, it would have softened the hearts of anyone except those two unfeeling brutes who held me in their sway. They did not say a word to me throughout the course of our journey, and I emulated their silence, allowing myself to be engulfed in my sorrow.

At eleven o'clock the following morning we arrived at a château that belonged to my eldest brother, situated in a deep wood somewhere between Coucy and Noyon.[4] The carriage entered the courtyard, and I was ordered to remain in it until the servants and horses were safely out of the way. At that point, my eldest brother came to fetch me.

"Follow me," he said brusquely, after having untied my hands and feet. Shaking from head to toe, I obeyed.

Good God, how can I describe to you how frightened I was when I saw the terrible place that was to serve as my place of detention. It was a low-ceilinged room, dark and dank, lighted only by a tiny window that looked down onto a large moat filled with water. The room, I noted, was barred on all sides.

"Here is where you are going to live, Mademoiselle," both my brothers said. "This is the kind of living quarters a daughter who dishonors her family deserves. Your food will be in proportion to the rest of your treatment. Here is what you will be given," they went on, producing for me to see a piece of dry bread of the kind given to animals, "and since on the one hand we don't want your suffering to be too long and drawn out, and on

the other we want to take whatever precautions are necessary to make sure you never leave here, these two
women"—and they gestured toward the old woman who
had accompanied us in the carriage and another one, who
could have passed for her double, whom we had seen
when we arrived at the château—"these two women
have been instructed to bleed you in both arms three
times a week, in keeping with the number of times you
went to visit Monsieur de *** at Berceil's house. Little
by little this regime will, or so we sincerely hope, lead
you to your grave, and we shall rest easy in our minds
only when we have been informed that the family is rid
of a monster such as yourself."

With these words, they ordered the women to seize
me and, in the presence of these two scoundrels—I hope
you will excuse my resorting to such a term, Monsieur—
they had me bled in both arms, only putting a stop to this
cruel operation when they saw I had lost consciousness.
When I came to my senses, I saw them congratulating
each other on their barbaric work, and as if they ex-
pressly wanted to make me bear all the slings of outrageous fortune simultaneously, as if they took special
pleasure in breaking my heart at the same time as they
were spilling my blood, the eldest brother pulled a letter
from his pocket and handed it to me.

"Here, Mademoiselle, read this and learn who is responsible for all your troubles."

With trembling fingers I tore open the envelope; my
eyes were scarcely strong enough for me to make out the
fatal handwriting: it was my lover's! It was he who had
betrayed me! Here is what that cruel letter said; the
words are still etched in blood in my heart.

I was foolish enough to fall in love with your sister, Monsieur, and had the audacity to dishonor her. I was on the verge of making amends, I had every intention of going and throwing myself at your father's feet, confessing my guilt, and asking for his daughter's hand. I was certain my own father would consent to the match, and I also felt that by my own birth and background I was full worthy of becoming a member of your family. But lo and behold, just as I had resolved to take this step, my eyes, my very own eyes, convinced me that I was dealing with nothing more than a whore, a woman who under the pretense of meeting me, motivated by the purest and most respectable of feelings, was using that cover to satisfy the unspeakable lusts of the most dissolute men. Therefore, do not expect me to make any further amends, for I owe you nothing. All I owe you is this: know that I shall never speak to her again and that I shall henceforth think of her only with the utmost hatred and the most profound contempt. I enclose with this letter the address of the house where your sister was wont to consummate her debauchery, so that you can verify that what I say is true.

No sooner had I finished reading these fateful words than I sank into the most terrible state of depression . . . "No," I said to myself, tearing my hair, "no, you heartless creature, you never loved me. If ever you had the slightest feeling for me, would you have let me be tried and sentenced without a hearing? Would you have believed me guilty of such a crime when it was you I adored? . . . O you false-hearted friend, to think that it was by your hand I was betrayed, by that same hand I was thrust into the arms of my torturers, whose intent is to kill me a little every day . . . to die without your ever knowing the truth . . . to die despised by the man I adore, the man whom I have never willingly offended, I who have been naught but the dupe and victim of other's wicked schemes . . . Oh, no, all this is too cruel, it is more than I can bear!" And throwing myself at my brothers' feet, I implored them to either hear my side of the story or put an end to this slow agony of daily bleeding and do away with me then and there.

They agreed to hear me out, and I told them the full story, sparing no detail, but they wanted me out of the way and not only did not believe a word I said but treated me all the more cruelly. After having then cursed me all the more roundly and having warned the two women that they were to carry out their order to the letter, under threat of death, they left me, remarking coldly that they hoped never to lay eyes on me again.

As soon as they had departed, my two jailers left with me my ration of bread and water and locked the door to my cell. But at least I was now alone and could give full vent to my despair, which somehow made me feel a trifle better. My first instinct, given my state of total despair, was to remove my bandages and let myself bleed to death. But the terrible notion that I would die without ever having been vindicated in the eyes of my lover struck me as so unacceptable that I could not bring myself to take that fatal step. A moment's peace brought a ray of hope . . . Hope, that comforting feeling that springs eternal in the midst of our deepest sorrows, that divine present with which Nature has endowed us to counterbalance or soften them . . . "No," I said to myself, "I refuse to die until I have seen him again, that is the goal I shall set for myself, I won't rest until I have achieved it.

If after he hears my side of the story he still thinks me guilty, than I shall be ready and willing to die, for I cannot conceive of a life without him, without his love."

Having made this decision, I resolved to do everything in my power to escape from these odious surroundings. For the next four days this resolution gave me a certain comfort, at which point my two jailers reappeared to bring me more bread and water and at the same time deprive me of the little strength I had left. Once again they bled me in both arms and left me prostrate on my bed. On the eighth day they reappeared and since I cast myself at their feet and asked them to spare me, they compromised by bleeding me from only one arm.

Two months went by in this manner, during which I was bled alternately in one arm or the other every four days. My strength of character worked in my favor, as did my relative youth. My unshakable desire to escape from this untenable situation, and the amount of bread I consumed to compensate for my exhaustion and enable me to carry out my resolutions, all that nursed me back to relative health, and by the beginning of the third month I managed to create a passage through the wall of my room, worm my way through the hole into a neighboring room that was unlocked, and, finally, escape from the château. I did my best to rejoin the road to Paris on foot when my strength gave out completely and I collapsed in the forest, where you found me and so generously came to my aid.

For that I am eternally grateful, Monsieur, and I beseech you to help me further by returning me to my father's care. For I have no doubt that he has been told a pack of lies, but I also know that he would never be so

cruel as to condemn me without giving me a proper hearing. I shall prove to him that, though I was indeed weak,
I am not as guilty as it might appear based on my brothers' false reports. And thanks to you, Monsieur, not only
will you have brought back to life a poor wretched creature who will be ever grateful to you as long as she lives,
but you will also have restored to a family the honor of
which it presently believes it has been unjustly deprived.

*　　*　　*

"Mademoiselle," said the Count de Luxeuil, after having listened attentively to Emilie's every word, "it is difficult to see you and hear you without caring deeply
about your fate. This said, while there is no doubt you
are not as guilty as people might be led to believe, your
behavior has been less than exemplary, which I'm sure
you yourself are the first to admit."

"Oh, Monsieur . . ."

"Hear me out, Mademoiselle, listen to the person
who, perhaps more than anyone else in the world, has
your best interests at heart. Your lover's behavior was un-
questionably ignoble. Not only is it unjust, for he was
honor-bound to see you and hear from your own lips a
full explanation, but it is also cruel. If a man reaches
a point when he decides he no longer wants to see a
woman with whom he's involved, he has the right to drop
her. But one does not denounce her to her own family,
one does not dishonor her, one does not shamelessly turn
her over to those intent on bringing about her ruin, nor
does one incite them to take their revenge . . . In other
words, I find the behavior of the man you purport to love

totally reprehensible. But your brothers' behavior is far more atrocious from every viewpoint: only butchers and torturers would behave so unspeakably. Misdeeds such as yours do not deserve such punishment. Chains have never served any useful purpose. In cases such as yours silence is the best remedy; but one does not bleed the guilty of their precious blood nor deprive them of their freedom. Such odious means dishonor far more those who impose them than those who are the victims; they deserve that person's hatred, they have stirred up a hornet's nest for no good reason and have done nothing to repair the presumed offense.[5] No matter how much we cherish a sister's virtue, her life has to be far more precious in our eyes. Honor can be repaired, but blood, once shed, can never be restored. So outrageous is their conduct that if one were to lodge a complaint against them with the authorities, they would doubtless be punished to the full extent of the law. But to resort to such means would debase us, bring us down to their level; what is more, it would only broadcast to the world at large what should better be kept under wraps. Therefore, we should by no means resort to such lowly tactics.

"I intend therefore to act in a totally different manner in order to serve your best interests, Mademoiselle, but I can only do so under the following conditions: first, that you provide me in writing your father's address, that of your aunt and of the Berceil woman, as well as the address of the place to which she took you; second, that you tell me clearly and candidly the name of the man you love. I shall go so far as to say that unless you divulge his name to me, it will be completely impossible to serve you in any way."

Emilie, confused and upset by the count's demands, nonetheless complied with his first request, and furnished him with the address of all three parties.

"Do you still require me to give you the name of my seducer?" she said, blushing.

"Absolutely, Mademoiselle," he responded. "Unless you do, there is nothing I can do to help."

"In that case his name is . . . the Marquis de Luxeuil . . ."

"The Marquis de Luxeuil!" the count cried out, scarcely able to conceal his emotions at the mention of his son's name. "You mean to tell me that that young rapscallion was capable of stooping so low!" Then, collecting himself, he said: "He will make amends, Mademoiselle, of that you may be sure. Take my word, you will have your revenge. *Adieu.*"

The extraordinary state of agitation that her final revelation had aroused in the count came as a complete surprise to poor Emilie, who was afraid she had committed some major indiscretion. And yet she found the count's words as he left her reassuring, and though she failed to understand how all these various elements fit into the picture or were somehow linked one to the other, she decided, since she had no way of figuring things out for herself, to patiently await the results of whatever steps her benefactor was taking. Meanwhile, the care for her health and welfare being lavished on her while the count was presumably setting things aright set her mind at rest and convinced her that people were indeed working in her best interests, that they had her happiness uppermost in their minds.

She had every reason to be even more convinced

when, four days after the revelations she had made, the count came into her room leading the Marquis de Luxeuil by the hand.

"Mademoiselle," he said, "I bring you in one and the same person both he who is responsible for your misfortunes and he who intends to make amends for them by begging you on bended knee to accept his offer for your hand."

With the words, the marquis cast himself at the feet of the woman he adored, but the surprise was too much for Emilie, who, still not strong enough to cope with such emotions, fainted dead away into the arms of her chambermaid. They administered to her, however, and she quickly regained her senses to find herself in her lover's arms.

"What a cruel man you are!" she began, a torrent of tears coursing down her cheeks, "what pain and suffering you caused the woman you said you loved! How could you ever think her capable of the infamous acts you dared suspect she had committed? Loving you as she did, Emilie may well have been guilty of her own weakness and a victim of the nefarious schemes of other people, but she would never have been unfaithful to you."

"O you whom I adore," the marquis cried out, "please, I beg of you to forgive my unpardonable jealousy, which I realize was based on false appearances. We all know now how unfounded they were, but in all fairness, didn't these fateful appearances indeed point a finger of guilt at you?"

"You should have had a higher opinion of me, Luxeuil, and if so you would not for a moment have believed that I could ever betray you. You should have heeded less your momentary despair and listened more to the feelings I flattered myself that I had inspired in you. May this example be a lesson to my sex, may it remember that it is almost always because we tend to love too much, because we yield too quickly, that we lose our lover's respect . . . O, Luxeuil, you would have esteemed me more if I had fallen in love with you less quickly. You made me pay for my weakness, and the very thing that should have cemented your love was what made you suspicious of mine."

"Let both of you put all that behind you," the count interrupted. "Luxeuil, your behavior is inexcusable, and if you hadn't offered to make immediate amends, if I had not sensed that your intentions were as honorable as they were sincere, I would never have set eyes on you again. All of which reminds me of that song sung by our ancient troubadours:

> When love is pure, when love is true if ever troubles do
> ensue
> By others' words or things they've seen that cast aspersions on your queen,
> Then listen not to what is said, but start to listen to
> your heart.[6]

"Mademoiselle," he went on, addressing himself to Emilie, "I am looking forward to your full and speedy recovery, for I want to return you to your family as my son's betrothed, and I flatter myself that they will not raise any objection in joining me to make amends for all your misfortunes. If for any reason they refuse my offer, then you should know that my house is yours, Mademoiselle, and it is here that we shall celebrate your marriage. Know too that, whether your family agrees to this marriage or not, I shall always think of you, to my dying day, as my cherished daughter, one with whom I consider it a great honor to be allied."

The young marquis embraced his father; Mademoiselle de Tourville burst into tears and clasped her benefactor's hands in hers. Both men withdrew for a few hours to allow Emilie to recover from a scene that had been both long and emotional. They did not want to be the cause of a setback to her complete recovery, which they desired with all their heart.

Precisely two weeks after her return to Paris, Mademoiselle de Tourville was strong enough to get up and take a carriage. The count had her dressed in a white dress in keeping with the innocence of her heart, every care was taken to enhance her natural beauty, which her lingering pallor and a remnant of her illness made all the more attractive. The count, his son, and Emilie drove together to her father's house. He, having not been forewarned of her visit, was completely taken aback when his daughter suddenly appeared. He was with his two sons, whose faces were immediately transformed into expressions of surprise and wrath. Both brothers were aware that she had escaped from the château, but they thought she had perished in some remote corner of the forest, and if they had the slightest remorse there was no visible evidence of it that one could detect.

"Monsieur," the count said as he presented Emilie to her father, "here is the very essence of innocence, which I return to your loving care . . . ," at which point Emilie threw herself at her father's feet. "I ask that she be forgiven," the count went on, "and I would not ask you this favor if I were not certain that she richly deserves it. Moreover," he continued, picking up the pace of his discourse, "the best proof I can give you of the profound esteem in which I hold your daughter is that I ask you for her hand in marriage to my son. We are of roughly equal stations in life," he said, "but if it turns out that my fortune is less than yours, then you may rest assured that I shall sell whatever of my goods and possessions it requires to provide my son with a fortune worthy of your daughter. It is for you to decide, Monsieur, and grant me leave not to depart until I have your word."

The elderly Judge de Tourville, who had always adored his darling Emilie, and who himself was goodness personified, so much so in fact that for the past twenty years he had retired from the bench precisely because of the excellence of his character,[7] the elderly judge, I say, letting his tears course down onto the bosom of his dear darling Emilie child, replied to the count that he was only too happy at the thought of such a match but that what bothered him and upset him no end was the fear that his darling Emilie might be unworthy. At which point the marquis cast himself at the judge's feet and asked the old man to forgive him for his own misdeeds and swore that he would atone for them.

Pledges were made on both sides, arrangements were discussed relative to the upcoming marriage, and emotions, which had been running high, abated. The only sour notes in the proceedings were Emilie's brothers, who refused to partake of the pervasive joy and who, when Emilie had gone over to embrace them, had not only pushed her away but turned to leave the room. The count, furious at their behavior, tried to stop one of the brothers from leaving the premises, but Monsieur de Tourville called out to him:

"Never mind, let them go. They have deceived me horribly. If this dear child of mine had been as guilty as they have made out, why then would you be at such pains to want her for your son's wife? By depriving me of my Emilie's cherished presence, they have unsettled my days and turned my former happiness into sorrow. Let them go . . ." And filled with rage, the brothers stalked from the room.

Then the count went on to recite for the judge the full litany of despicable acts that his sons had visited upon his daughter. The judge, upset and dismayed by the total disproportion between the deed and the punishment, swore that he would never set eyes on his sons again. The count tried to smooth things over and made the judge promise to wipe all this unpleasantness from his memory.

A week later, the marriage took place without the presence of the two sons, who refused to honor their father's invitation. But the ceremony unfolded very smoothly without them and they both were held in great contempt by all concerned. Monsieur de Tourville decided not to take legal action against them, warning them, however, to keep their mouths shut, adding that if they refused he would have them locked up. They did more or less as he had bidden, but they could not refrain from boasting about what they had done without being specific, then complaining to one and all that their father was far too lenient with their sister.

People who became privy to the frightful details of

this unfortunate misadventure were appalled by it, shaking their heads and saying:

"Good God! This is one appalling example of what can happen when private individuals take it into their heads to punish crimes committed by others![8] How right people are when they maintain that such infamous conduct is the preserve of the crazed, incompetent devotees of blind justice, of Themis herself. Brought up in a climate of ridiculous inflexibility, their hearts hardened at the most tender age against the cries of the poor and downtrodden, their hands bloodied from the cradle, harsh in their judgments of others but lenient to a fault when it comes to their own behavior, firm in their conviction that the only way to keep their own vices secret and cover up their public prevarications is by flaunting their unbending nature, these future judges have the outward appearance of a lion and the inner character of a goose. Their only purpose, even as they steep themselves in crime, is to pull the wool over the eyes of the gullible and make wise men loathe not only their odious principles and their bloodthirsty laws, but their own detestable persons."

AUGUSTINE DE VILLEBLANCHE or LOVE'S STRATEGY

"O
f all Nature's aberrations, the one that has caused
the most controversy and seemed the strangest to
those semi-philosophers who spend their lives analyzing
everything without ever understanding anything," said
Mademoiselle de Villeblanche (with whom we shall later
have an opportunity to converse) to one of her closest female friends, "is this strange penchant that women of a
certain disposition and temperament have for persons of
their own sex. Although long before and since the time
of the immortal Sappho[1] every country in the world, and
indeed every city, has produced women of this bent, and
although in the face of this overwhelming evidence it
would seem reasonable to accuse Nature of eccentricity
rather than accuse these women of unnatural crimes, the
fact remains that we have never ceased to blame and
censure them. And if it were not for the haughty sup-
eriority that our sex has always enjoyed, who knows
whether some Cujas, some Bartolo, or some Louis IX[2]
might not have conceived the idea of punishing these
sensitive and unhappy creatures by burning them at

the stake, as they have felt obliged to do with men who, possessed of this same penchant and doubtless for as compelling reasons, have thought it possible to find satisfaction among members of their own sex and held the opinion that congress between the two sexes, while essential for the propagation of the race, might well not be of such overriding importance when it comes to the pursuit of pleasure. God forbid that we should take sides in this dispute, don't you agree, my dear?" the beautiful Augustine de Villeblanche continued, as she blew kisses, which nonetheless seemed slightly suspicious, in the direction of her charming friend. "But instead of resorting to the use of sarcasm or scorn, or the threat of the stake— weapons which hardly seem meaningful today—would it not be infinitely simpler, in a matter so completely indifferent to society, of absolutely no consequence to God, and perhaps even more useful to Nature than we tend to realize, to let everyone do as he or she pleases? . . . What is there to fear from this depravity? . . . In the eyes of any truly wise person, it will seem that it may well prevent more serious ones, but no one will ever make me believe that it can lead to more dangerous deviant behavior . . . Ah, good heaven, are they afraid that the whims of these individuals of one or the other sex will bring about the end of the world, that they are playing games with the ever-so-precious human race, and that their so-called crime will wipe it out, since they are failing to assure it grows and multiplies? If you think about it carefully, you will see that all these imaginary losses are completely indifferent to Nature, that not only does she not condemn them but, on the contrary, she demonstrates by a thousand examples that she wishes and desires them. Why, if these losses irritate her so, would she tolerate them in thousands of cases? Why, if the problem of progeny is so essential to her, would she have limited the length of time a woman can bear children to only a third of her life? And why would Nature dictate that half of those creatures to whom she gives birth leave their mothers' hands with a clear distaste for producing offspring, contrary to what we have been taught are Nature's demands. I shall go even further: Nature allows the race to multiply, but she does not demand it and, thoroughly convinced that there will always be more people than her needs require, she has no desire whatsoever to oppose the penchants of those who refuse to conform to society's demands to procreate and will have no part of it. Ah, let Mother Nature work her ways, let us be quite convinced that her resources are immense, that nothing we do will outrage her, and that we humans are not equipped to commit any crime that will affect or endanger her laws."

Mademoiselle de Villeblanche, a sample of whose logic we have just seen, was at the age of twenty in full control of her own life. Blessed with an income of thirty thousand francs, she had decided that she was not made for marriage. She came from a good, though not illustrious, family. She was the only child of a man who had made his fortune in India and died without ever having been able to persuade her to marry. We would be less than candid if we did not reveal that the kind of penchant for which Augustine had just offered such a vigorous defense played a major role in her aversion to marriage. Whatever the reason—whether it was advice received, education, predisposition, her own hot blood (she was born in Madras), Nature's inspiration, or any

other reason you can think of—Mademoiselle de Villeblanche detested men and, totally dedicated to what
chaste ears will understand by the term "sapphism,"
found pleasure only with members of her own sex and
compensated for her contempt of Love only with the
Graces.[3]

Augustine was a real loss to men: tall, statuesque,
she had beautiful dark hair, a slightly aquiline nose, su-
perb teeth, eyes that sparkled with intelligence and wit;
and her skin was exquisitely smooth and white; in a
word, she emanated an aura of such piquant voluptuous-
ness that it came as no surprise that a number of men,
seeing her so perfectly made to give love and so determined not to receive it, quite naturally let slip an infinite
number of sarcastic remarks about a taste which, however simple it may have been, nonetheless deprived the
altars of Paphos[4] of one of the creatures best endowed to
serve them and thus caused a certain degree of ill humor
among the adepts of the temples of Venus. Mademoiselle de Villeblanche shrugged off these reproaches and
all the malicious gossip about her with a good-natured
laugh, and went right on indulging in her own caprices.

"The most foolish thing of all," she used to say, "is
to blush about the penchants that Nature has given us.
And to make fun of anyone, simply because his or her
tastes are unusual, is just as barbaric as railing against
someone who was born lame, or blind in one eye. But
trying to convince fools of these reasonable concepts is
like trying to halt the stars in their courses. People seem
to take a kind of prideful pleasure in mocking defects
that they themselves do not possess, and they apparently
derive such enjoyment—especially the halfwits—from

this sport, that it is very rare to see them give it up . . . It serves as a pretext for maliciousness, witticisms, and poor puns; and society, that is, a collection of people whom boredom has brought together and stupidity has molded, enjoys nothing better than spending two or three hours talking without saying anything, it delights in appearing brilliant at the expense of others, in making a point of censuring a vice from which it thinks itself free . . . This is a slightly roundabout way of patting yourself on the back. By the same token, people even agree to join forces with others to form a clique and crush the individual whose major sin is not to conform like everyone else, and they go home feeling proud as peacocks for the wit they have shown, whereas all they have basically proved by their conduct, when you come right down to it, is their own pedantry and stupidity."

Such were Mademoiselle de Villeblanche's thoughts. Having firmly decided never to hold her feelings in check, caring not a whit for what people said about her, wealthy enough to provide for her own requirements, unconcerned about her reputation, desiring a sybaritic life, one of luxury and pleasure rather than one filled with heavenly beatitudes in which she scarcely believed, believing even less in any kind of immortality which, to her mind, sounded all too chimerical, surrounded by a small circle of kindred souls, Augustine gave herself over in all innocence to every pleasure that touched her fancy.

She had had more than her share of suitors, but she had treated them all so shabbily that any hope of ever winning her heart had virtually been abandoned when there appeared on the scene a young man named Franville, whose background was more or less equal to hers and who was at least as rich as she. He fell madly in love with her, and not only was he not put off by the tales of her inflexibility but made up his mind then and there that he would not give up until the conquest was his. He confided his plan to his friends, they told him he was mad, he maintained that he would succeed, they challenged him to prove it, and he accepted the bet. Franville was two years younger than Mademoiselle de Villeblanche, had as yet scarcely any show of beard, was possessed of a fine figure, the most delicate features, and the most beautiful head of hair in the world. In fact, when he dressed as a girl he looked so well in feminine attire that he was forever fooling both sexes, with the result that he had often received both from those who were taken in as well as those who knew his true identity, propositions so clearly framed that he could easily have become, in the course of the same day, some Hadrian's Antinoüs or some Psyche's Adonis.[5] It was with this costume that Franville fancied he would be able to seduce Mademoiselle de Villeblanche. We shall shortly see how he went about it.

One of Augustine's greatest pleasures was to dress up as a man during carnival and, in this disguise so inconsistent with her tastes, flit from one party to the next. Franville, who had had her watched and followed and who, up to this time, had made a point of keeping out of her sight as much as possible, learned one day that she would be attending a masked ball that same evening given by the patrons of the Opera, and that she would, as usual, be dressed up as a man, that evening as a captain of dragoons. He disguised himself as a woman, taking great pains with his makeup and dress to appear as elegant as possible, with liberal applications of rouge and no mask. Then, taking in tow one of his sisters who was far less attractive than he, he hied himself to the gathering, to which Augustine was going only to see who she could pick up.

Before Franville had finished circling the room three times, Augustine's knowing eyes had singled him out.

"Who is that beautiful young lady?" she said to the girl she was with. "I don't remember ever seeing her before. How could we have missed such a gorgeous creature?"

And no sooner had she uttered these words than Augustine made every effort to strike up a conversation with the false Mademoiselle de Franville, who at first fled from her advances, turned his back, snubbed her, avoided her, all of which merely to make himself more ardently desired. Finally Augustine cornered him, they exchanged a few banalities, but little by little the conversation became more interesting.

"It's frightfully warm in here," said Mademoiselle de Villeblanche. "Our friends can stay here, but why don't we go over to the game rooms, where they serve refreshments, and get a breath of fresh air."

"Ah, Monsieur," said Franville to Mademoiselle de Villeblanche, still pretending to take her for a man, "I'm only here with my sister, but my mother will be along shortly with the man I'm meant to marry, and if either one of them were to see us together there's no telling what kind of trouble . . ."

"Come, come, you must learn to overcome these childish fears. How old are you, my angel?"

"Eighteen, Monsieur."

"Ah! And I say by the time one has reached the age of eighteen one should have the right to do whatever one chooses . . . Come, now, I won't take no for an answer. Follow me, and have no fear . . ." And Franville followed meekly in her footsteps.

"Do you really mean to tell me, you charming creature," Augustine went on, as she led the person she still mistook for a young woman toward the gambling rooms adjacent to the main ballroom, "do you mean to tell me that you really are going to get married? . . . I must say I pity you . . . And who is this person they've chosen for you? A real bore, I'd be willing to wager . . . Ah, what a lucky man he is, and what I wouldn't give to be in his place! Tell me, you heavenly child, would you consent to marry me if you had the chance? I want an honest answer!"

"What can I say, Monsieur? You know as well as I that when you are young you have little choice but to follow the dictates of your heart."

"But you can still refuse your hand to this wretched fellow. Give us time to get to know each other better and if everything works out to our mutual satisfaction why couldn't we come to some sort of understanding? I, thank God, don't have to ask anyone for permission. Although I'm only twenty, I'm the master of my own fortune, and if you could talk to your parents on my behalf, I see no reason why we could not be united in holy wedlock before the week is out!"

As they talked, they had left the ballroom, and the clever Augustine, who was not leading her prey there to spend their time on idle chatter, had been careful to take her into one of those isolated rooms which she, through her prior arrangements with those who organized these affairs, always managed to have at her disposal.

"Oh, God!" said Franville as soon as he saw Augustine close the door behind her and try to take him in her arms. "What in heaven's name are you trying to do? What do you mean, bringing me here alone with you, Monsieur, to such an out-of-the-way spot? Let me go, let me go this minute or, I swear to you, I'll call for help."

"I'm going to prevent you from calling anyone, my sweet angel," said Augustine, planting her lovely lips squarely on Franville's. "Now cry for help, cry for help if you can, but I warn you that the fragrance of your rose-scented breath will only be more prompt to inflame my heart."

Franville made a half-hearted effort to defend himself: it's difficult to be very angry when you are in the throes of receiving, as tenderly as he was, the first kiss of the person you adore. Encouraged, Augustine pressed on her attack with renewed vigor, with the kind of vehemence particular only to those delightful women compelled by this fantasy. It was not long before her hands began to wander, Franville meanwhile playing the role of the woman who is yielding and whose hands, almost unconsciously, respond by groping in turn. Clothes are pushed aside, and almost at the same moment their fingers reach the spot where each expects to find what he or she is expectantly looking for . . . At which point Franville suddenly switched roles:

"What in the name of . . ." he cried out. "You mean to tell me you're only a *woman!* . . ."

"You horrible creature," Augustine retorted, her hand enveloping things the very condition of which destroyed her every illusion, "you mean to tell me I've gone to all this trouble over a poor miserable man . . . I must be the most unlucky woman alive."

"No more than me, if you want to know the truth," said Franville, straightening his clothes and making a show of the most profound disdain. "I use this disguise for cruising, it is men I am looking for and men alone I love. And all I find is a twopenny whore . . ."

"Whore indeed!" said Augustine bitterly. "I have never been a whore in my life, and the mere fact that I loathe men is no reason to treat me this way . . ."

"What! You're a woman and you hate men?"

"Yes, and for the exact same reason that you're a man and hate women."

"A rather unique meeting, at least I can say that much for it."

"And a sad one for me, too," said Augustine, displaying all the symptoms of ill humor.

"The truth is, Mademoiselle, that this is far more irksome for me than it is for you," Franville said bitterly. "Here I am contaminated for three weeks. Do you know that in our order we take a vow never to touch a woman?"

"It seems to be that one could touch someone like me without disgracing oneself."

"Upon my word, my dear girl," Franville went on, "I can't see any great reason why you should be an exception, and I fail to see how a vice should give you any special merit."

"A vice! . . . Who do you think you are, talking to me about my vice when you admit to such an unspeakable one yourself!"

"There's no point in arguing, is there?" said Franville. "Two can play at that game. The simplest thing would be to go our own ways and never see each other again."

And so saying Franville reached over to open the door.

"Not so fast," said Augustine, "not so fast," preventing him from opening the doors. "I gather you intend to broadcast our little adventure to the entire world."

"I may, if it amuses me."

"What do I care, for that matter. Thank God I'm above such gossip. Go ahead, Monsieur, leave and say anything you like . . ." But once again she stopped him from leaving. "Do you know what," she said with a smile, "this is quite a remarkable tale. It was not just one of us, but *both* of us who made a mistake."

"Ah! But the error is far more painful to people such as me than it is to your kind . . . You have no idea how revolting we find this . . . this emptiness."

"You don't say! You can take my word for it, my dear fellow, that what you offer us in its place is no less repugnant to us, the disgust is mutual. But you have to admit, this adventure is rather amusing . . . Are you going back to the ball?"

"I don't know."

"Well, I'm not," said Augustine. "I'm far too upset—disagreeably, thanks to you. I'm going home."

"Good for you!"

"But I wonder whether the gentleman might be civil enough to escort me there. I live but a stone's throw away, and don't have my carriage. He can leave me at my doorstep."

"Of course he will. I'll be happy to take you," Franville said. "Our different tastes shouldn't keep us from being polite. May I offer you my arm? . . . There."

"The only reason I'm accepting your offer is that I haven't found a better one."

"And you may rest assured that the only reason I'm offering you my arm is out of a basic sense of decency."

They reached the door to Augustine's house, and Franville prepared to take his leave.

"I must say, you are quite charming," said Mademoiselle de Villeblanche. "What? You're going to leave me here in the street?"

"I'm terribly sorry," Franville mumbled. "I didn't dare . . ."

"Ah, how churlish, you men who don't like women!"

"It's only that," said Franville by way of explanation, nonetheless offering his arm to Mademoiselle de Villeblanche and accompanying her to her door, "it's only that I was in a hurry to get back to the ball, Mademoiselle, to try to make amends for my stupid mistake."

"Your stupid mistake! You mean you're all that angry at having met me?"

"I didn't say that, Mademoiselle, but given who we are, don't you agree we could both have found infinitely better partners?"

"Yes, you're right," Augustine said, as she finally opened her door and went in, "you're right, Monsieur, especially where I'm concerned . . . Because I'm very much afraid that this fatal encounter may cost me my happiness."

"What do you mean? Aren't you absolutely certain of your feelings?"

"I was yesterday."

"Ah! You're not bound by your principles."

"I'm bound by nothing . . . You're beginning to weary me."

"Then let me take my leave, Mademoiselle, by all means let me be on my way. God forbid I should disturb you another moment."

"No, stay. I order you to stay. Can't you for once in your life accept to obey a woman?"

"There's nothing I can't do," Franville responded, promptly obliging by sitting down. "As I told you, I'm a decent sort."

"Do you realize how terrible it is for someone like you to have such perverse tastes?"

"And do you think it's any more respectable for you to have the bizarre tastes that are yours?"

"Ah, for us it's quite different. It's a question of modesty, of caution . . . or of pride if you prefer, the fear of having to submit to your sex, whose only purpose in seducing us is to dominate . . . Still, our carnal urges cannot be denied and we manage to arrange things quite easily among ourselves. Assuming we are discreet, no one is one whit the wiser: we display a veneer of respectability to the world, which most people accept. Thus the demands of Nature are satisfied, decency is observed, and modesty is not outraged."

"Now there's as fine a set of good, solid sophisms as I've ever heard. Applying them to whatever purpose, one could justify anything. What's more, what have you said that could not also be cited in our favor?"

"Not in the least! Your prejudices are quite different from ours, our fears are something quite foreign to you.

What is victory for you is defeat for us. The more conquests you make, the greater your glory. And the only way you can control the feelings we arouse in you are through vice and depravity."

"Truly, I do believe you are going to convert me."

"Would that I could."

"But pray, what would you gain by so doing, as long as you're mired in the error of your own ways?"

"My sex would be grateful to me. And since I love women, I'm only too happy to work on their behalf."

"If by chance the miracle were to happen, its effects would not be as general as you seem to think. I would like to be converted for only one woman at the very most . . . as a kind of test case."

"'Tis an honorable desire."

"What is certain beyond all doubt is that to take a stance without having actually undergone the experience smacks of prejudice."

"What? You've never been with a woman?"

"Never! And you . . . would you by chance be as pure on your end as I am in mine?"

"Oh, pure . . . I'm not sure that's the right word . . . The women we are involved with are so clever and so jealous that they leave nothing undiscovered . . . But as for men, no, I've never had a man in my life."

"You swear to that?"

"Nor do I ever want to see, or ever to know, a man with tastes as bizarre as mine."

"I'm only sorry I didn't make the same vow myself."

"I don't believe I've ever heard anything more impertinent in my life!"

Saying which, Mademoiselle de Villeblanche got to her feet and informed Franville he was free to leave. Our young lover, utterly cool, calm, and collected, bowed deeply and prepared to depart.

"I suppose you're going back to the ball," Mademoiselle de Villeblanche said dryly, casting a glance in his direction that was a mixture of utter disdain and hopeless ardent love.

"Why, yes. As I believe I've already mentioned."

"In other words, you're incapable of making the sacrifice for me that I have made for you?"

"I beg your pardon. Just what sacrifice would you be referring to?"

"I came home only because I had no desire to stay at the ball after I had the misfortune of meeting you."

"The misfortune?"

"You're the one who forces me to use that expression. And it's you and you alone who have the power to make me use another."

"And how are you going to reconcile that with your own tastes?"

"When love o'ertakes, tastes relegate."

"That may well be, but you could never possibly love me."

"I agree, not so long as you practice those frightful habits I learned were yours."

"And what if I forswore them?"

"Then I would immediately reciprocate by sacrificing my own on the altar of love . . . Oh, you faithless creature. Do you realize what that confession does to my pride? Do you have the faintest notion what you have just forced me to say?" she said, collapsing into a chair, tears streaming down her cheeks.

"The confession I heard, from the most beautiful lips in the world, is the most flattering any man could ever hope to hear," said Franville, casting himself at Augustine's feet. "Oh, my love, my dear, sweet love. I have to confess this was all a ploy on my part. Do not punish me for it, I beg of you on bended knee, do forgive me. I shall stay here until you do! You see before you, Mademoiselle, the most steadfast, the most passionate of lovers. I felt I had to resort to this ruse to win over a heart I knew to be hard and unyielding. Have I succeeded, dear Augustine? Will you spurn the untainted love that you deigned to accept for a guilty lover, for one as guilty as I . . . guilty at least in your own mind. Oh! Did you for a minute think that any impure passion could dwell in the soul of one who loves only you?"

"Of all the dirty, lowdown tricks! You were leading me on the whole time! But yes, I do forgive you! . . . And yes, now that I think about it, you're not giving up anything for me, which is a blow to my pride, while I'm ready to give up everything for you. Well, so be it . . . I'm only too happy to renounce the error of my ways for you—errors into which vanity leads us almost as often as does our own tastes. I feel that Nature is winning out, that same Nature I suppressed through my own foibles and failings, which I hereby abhor and renounce with all my heart. Her power is irresistible. She has created us for you and you alone, as she has created you men for us. Let us yield to her laws. It is through love itself that Nature inspires me to obey them today and it is love, too, that will etch them more deeply in my heart.

"Here, Sir, is my hand. I believe you to be a man of honor, and true worthy as a suitor. If for a moment I fell low in your esteem, know that I shall do everything in my power, through affection and loving care, to make amends for whatever wrongs I may have done, as I shall oblige you to acknowledge that such wrongs, emanating from too ardent an imagination, do not necessarily debase a well-born soul."

Franville, having achieved his cherished goal, let loose a torrent of tears of joy onto the fair hands that he was covering with a thousand kisses. Then he rose and threw himself into Augustine's open arms. "This is the happiest day of my life," he cried. "There is nothing to compare to my victory. I have brought back to the path of virtue a straying heart wherein I shall reign forever."

Franville showered a thousand kisses upon the divine object of his love, then departed. The following day he informed all his friends of his good fortune. Mademoiselle de Villeblanche was far too good a match for his parents to refuse their consent, and within a week they were married.

Affection, trust, utter devotion, and extreme modesty were the marks of their marriage, and by making himself the happiest of men he was sufficiently astute to turn the most libertine of young women into the most chaste and virtuous of wives.

THE FORTUNATE RUSE

*T*here are any number of wives so foolish as to think
that, just as long as their husband does not surprise
them *flagrante delicto* with a lover, they can at least indulge in a fair amount of amorous dalliance without of-
fending their lawful-wedded spouse. As it turns out, that
point of view often has consequences more dangerous
than if the betrayal had actually been consummated.
What happened to the Marquise de Guissac, a lady of
quality from Nîmes in the Languedoc region of southern
France, offers a concrete example of that general truth.

A bit on the giddy side, a happy-go-lucky person
who sometimes acted first and thought later, she was as
full of wit as her heart was kind. Madame de Guissac believed that a handful of love letters exchanged between
her and the Baron d'Aumelas would have no serious consequences; first because no one would ever be the wiser
about them and second because, in the unlikely event
they ever did come to light, she would have no trouble
explaining them to her husband, thus exonerating her,
since in fact she was blameless in her husband's eyes.
But she was badly mistaken.

Monsieur de Guissac, who was excessively jealous,
suspected that something was going on between these

two. He questioned a chambermaid, and fell upon one of their letters. At first glance, there was nothing in that letter to incriminate her outright, but more than enough to feed his suspicions. "Doubt, doubt, damnable doubt," he muttered to himself. And armed with a goblet of lemonade in one hand and a loaded pistol in another, he burst into his wife's bedroom.

"I am betrayed!" he shouted, clearly beside himself with anger. "Read this letter. It tells me more than I need to know. Enough of this shilly-shallying. I leave it up to you: you can choose the way you want to die."

The marquise spoke up in her own defense, swearing to her husband that he was making a terrible mistake, that she may well have been guilty of acting imprudently but certainly not of any crime.

"You've betrayed me for the last time," he said, still livid, "and you can be sure you will never betray me again. I repeat: you can choose how you want to die or this pistol will end your days here and now." And he pushed the goblet toward her.

Poor Madame Guissac, beside herself with fear, seized the goblet, which she knew was laced with poison, and began to drink.

"Stop!" her husband said as soon as he saw that she had swallowed a portion of the lethal liquid. "You're not going to die alone. Despised by you, betrayed by you, what do you think will become of me once you are gone?"

And with those words, he seized the chalice and downed the rest of its contents.

"Oh, Sir," Madame de Guissac cried out, "in the frightful state to which you have reduced us both, grant me the right at least to see a confessor and at the same time to embrace my mother and father one last time."

Servants were dispatched forthwith to summon those whom the poor woman had asked for, and when her parents arrived she threw herself into the arms of those who had brought her into this world and once again stoutly proclaimed her innocence. But what words of reproach could be heaped upon a husband who, believing he had been betrayed, had so cruelly punished his wife but also meted out the same punishment to himself? All they could do was to vent their despair, and tears flowed freely on all sides.

At which point the father confessor arrived.

"At this cruel moment of my life," she said to him, "I wish to make a full and frank confession, both to bring comfort to my dear parents and for the honor of my own memory." Saying which, she proceeded to unburden her conscience of all the sins, large and small, she had committed since the day she was born.

Her husband, hanging on her every word and certain that at such a crucial point in her life she would not conceal the slightest misdeed, heard not the least mention of the Baron d'Aumelas and was overcome with joy. He got to his feet and said, as he clasped first her mother then her father to his breast:

"Dear, dear parents, you have heard your daughter's reassuring words. May she pardon me for giving her such a fright. But the fact is, she gave me so much cause for concern that I feel justified in giving her a bit in return. There was no poison in the cup we both drank from. Only lemonade. So, my love, put your mind at rest, let us put all our minds at rest. But let it be a lesson to us all: a woman should be truly honorable in all respects, not only in deeds but in words. She should, to quote the bard, always be above suspicion."

The marquise, thoroughly convinced by the force of her imagination that she had really drunk poison from the goblet, had a great deal of difficulty recovering her wits, for she was actually suffering the physical and mental anguish of death by poisoning. She struggled to her feet, still shaking like a leaf, and embraced her husband. Pain gave way to joy and the young woman, unduly punished by the terrible experience, swore that in the future she would avoid even the vaguest semblance of wrong-doing.

And she was true to her word. For more than thirty years she lived in perfect harmony with her husband, and during all that time he never found anything in her conduct that was worthy of the slightest reproach.

THE PROPERLY
PUNISHED PIMP

*D*uring the Regency,[1] an adventure so extraordinary occurred that it still bears repeating, and may even prove enlightening in the context of today's world. On the one hand it tells of a secret debauchery on which light deserves to be shed. On the other, it is a tale of three brutal murders, the author of which was never found. But before we relate the gory details of the catastrophe itself, let us offer some conjectures about what happened, and show how events leading up to it may well have justified the result. By so doing, the ending may be less frightening.

Rumor has it that Monsieur Savari, whom Nature had not treated kindly,* though a confirmed bachelor, was nonetheless a man of wit and considerable social grace. He regularly entertained, in his house on the rue des Déjeuners,[2] people of the highest standing. For whatever reason, he had taken it into his head to turn his house into a setting for a most unusual kind of prostitution. He limited his invited guests to women of quality,

---

*He was a cripple, having been born legless.

both married and unmarried, who wished to enjoy with impunity the pleasures of the flesh in surroundings of the utmost discretion, knowing they could count on him to provide them with suitable partners ready and able to satisfy their desires. They knew, too, that there would be no untoward consequences of these fleeting intrigues, from which a woman can gather roses without fear of the thorns with which all too many of these arrangements are fraught, if ever they come to light and are viewed as lasting liaisons. A married woman, or a young lady, might at some social gathering the next day run into the man with whom she had had an affair the evening before without appearing to recognize him and without his taking any more notice of her than of any of the other women there. The result of all this: no scenes of jealousy among married couples, no fathers in a state of deep distress, no separation, no women hustled off to convents: in short, none of the unpleasantries to which this sort of affair can often lead. It is hard to imagine a more satisfactory arrangement, though I hasten to add that today it would in all likelihood be extremely dangerous. In a century where depravity not only rules the roost—and I include in that statement both sexes—but indeed knows virtually no bounds, it would doubtless be a matter of the gravest concern to think of reintroducing the practice unless at the same time we described in full detail the cruel fate that befell the gentleman who dreamed it up.

Although he was quite well off, Monsieur Savari, the originator and perpetrator of the project, limited himself to a single valet and a cook to keep the witnesses of the events taking place under his roof to a strict minimum.

One morning a man Savari knew arrived to ask if he might be invited to lunch.

"With great pleasure," Savari said, "and to show how pleased I am you've come I'm going to send my valet down to fetch a bottle of the finest wine in my cellar."

After the valet, whose name was La Brie,[3] had been given his instructions, the friend said: "You know what? I know your wine cellar like the back of my hand. I'm going to follow La Brie down there and make sure he's really bringing up the very best."

"Fine with me," said the master of the house, enjoying his friend's little joke, "if it weren't for my damn infirmity I'd go with you myself. But do go down and see to it the knave isn't cheating me."

The friend left the room and went down to the cellar, where he picked up a crowbar and dashed out the valet's brains, following which he went back upstairs and into the kitchen, where he meted out the same punishment to the cook, even going so far as to kill both a dog and cat he chanced upon on his way back to Savari's living quarters. His host, whose crippled state left him defenseless, suffered the same fate as had his servants. The pitiless murderer, who seemed completely unruffled and showed not the slightest twinge of remorse over the acts he had just committed, used the blank page of a book that happened to be on the table to calmly describe, in full detail, what he had just done. After which he did not touch another thing, removed nothing from the house, departed, locked the door behind him, and vanished.

Savari's house was too well frequented for this cruel slaughter to go undiscovered for very long. Various people came knocking on his door, and when there was no response, knowing the master of the house could not have gone out, they broke in and were greeted by the frightful carnage of the poor man's entire household.

The cold-blooded murderer, not content with having left for all the world to read the full details of his act, had placed over the face of a clock—which was decorated with a death's head and bore the maxim: *Look upon this and regulate your life*—a sheet of paper, on which he had written, then pasted just below the maxim, the following:

> If you see how he lived you will not be surprised by his death.

Naturally, such a crime soon became known far and wide. A thorough investigation ensued, but the only apparent piece of evidence they came up with was an unsigned letter from a woman writing to Monsieur Savari, which went:

> We are lost! My husband has just found out everything! The only person who can turn him around is Paparel. You must get Paparel to talk to him, otherwise there is no hope for either of us.

There was indeed a man named Paparel who worked in the war office, a man highly ranked in the paymaster's department, who was known to be a kind and gentle creature, and a man of excellent credentials. Nonetheless, he was summoned, and while he admitted to having a nodding acquaintance with Savari, he maintained that among the hundred or so personages of both the court and the city who were known to be friends of the deceased, foremost among them the Duke de Vendôme,[4] he, Paparel, knew the man the least.

Several people were arrested but were released almost immediately. But the authorities did glean enough from their investigations to convince themselves that there were countless ramifications to this offense, which while implicating half the fathers and husbands in the capital, were also going to involve an infinite number of people in the highest echelons of society. And for the first time in their lives, prudence took precedence over severity in the minds of the magistrates. And so the matter remained. As a result, the death of this poor fellow was not only never solved but also never avenged. Doubtless he was guilty enough so that proper, upstanding people did not shed a tear over his passing. But if his death in no wise added to the world's store of Virtue, it is to be believed that Vice mourned his loss for a very long time indeed, and that, independently of the merry band of rakes who had, within the welcoming walls of this disciple of Epicurus, gathered so many of love's blossoms, the pretty priestesses of Venus who, on the altars, had daily come to burn the incense of love, must have mourned the demolition of their temple just as greatly.

Thus are all things measured one against the other.

Upon reading this account, a philosopher would doubtless say:

> If out of a thousand people who may have been implicated in this affair, 500 were pleased by its outcome and 500 displeased, one would call it neutral, a draw.

But if on the other hand 800 were greatly distressed by the fact that the catastrophe had deprived them of their former pleasures, against, say, 200 who were pleased by the man's disappearance, then one would be obliged to conclude that Monsieur Savari did more good than evil, and the only guilty party was he who, doubtless to avenge himself, had committed the crime.

I leave it to you to decide and move quickly on to another subject.

THE TEACHER PHILOSOPHER

*A*mong all the learned matters one tries to cram into a child's head when one is in charge of his education, the mysteries of Christianity, though doubtless one of the most sublime elements of that education, are nonetheless not among the easiest to explain clearly to a young mind. Try to convince a young man of fourteen or fifteen, for instance, that God the Father and God the Son are one and the same, that the Father is consubstantial to the Son and vice versa, etc., all that, however necessary it may be in ensuring a person's happiness here below, is far more difficult to make a person understand than it is, say, to teach someone algebra. And when you really want to get your point across in a meaningful way, it is sometimes necessary to resort to physical examples, certain concrete methods that, however disproportionate they may seem, nonetheless make it easier for a young man of reasonable intelligence to grasp.

No one was more profoundly practiced in this method of instruction than Abbé Du Parquet, tutor to the young Count de Nerceuil, who was about fifteen years of age and possessed of one of the handsomest faces imaginable.

"Father," the young count was wont to say virtually

every day to his tutor, "the truth is, the whole notion of consubstantiality is completely beyond my powers of comprehension. For the life of me, I just can't figure out how two people can be one. Could you be kind enough to clarify this for me, or at least bring the mystery down to my level."

The good abbé, anxious to leave no stone unturned in making sure his student's education was complete, and pleased by the thought that he might make it easier for his student to comprehend anything that might someday be an important factor in his life, seized upon a rather pleasurable means of overcoming the difficulties the young count was having in understanding the concept, figuring that an example taken from real life might just do the trick. Accordingly, he had a young nubile girl brought forth and after having instructed her as to what was expected of her, conjoined, as it were, the girl and his young student.

"Now," said the abbé to his student, "do you understand more clearly the mystery of consubstantiality? Do you see how it is quite possible for two people to be but one?"

"Oh, good heavens, yes, my dear Abbé," the randy young count responded, "I now understand everything with amazing clarity. Nor am I any longer surprised if this mystery, so people maintain, provides as much pleasure as that reserved for those in heaven above, for when two people become one 'tis pure pleasure, I find."

A few days later the young count asked his tutor if he wouldn't mind giving him another lesson, for the more he thought about it the more he realized, he said, that he had not fully plumbed the depths of the mystery but that he was sure that if he tried it one more time everything would become crystal clear. The obliging abbé, who had in all likelihood been just as amused by the scene he had concocted as his student had been, called the same girl back and the second lesson got under way. But this time the abbé, especially moved by the vision offered to him by the sight of young de Nerceuil as he was consubstantiating with his companion, could not refrain from involving himself as a third party interested in the further clarification of the evangelical parable, and the beauteous backside upon which his hands were compelled to roam in the process of his explanation ended up exciting him uncontrollably.

"It is my studied opinion," said Du Parquet, "that things are progressing at far too fast a pace. Much too much buoyancy in all the movements, as a result of which the conjunction, not being as intimate as it ought to be, does not conjure up a proper image of the mystery. Let me demonstrate . . . If we set about it just so, this way . . ." whereupon the scoundrel did unto his student precisely what the student was doing unto the young lady.

"Oh! Good God above! you're hurting me, Abbé," the lad exclaimed. "Nor can I see that this whole ceremony is serving any useful purpose. In what way, may I ask, does this further clarify the mystery?"

"Oh, *ventrebleu!*"[1] the abbé mumbled, overcome as he was by the pleasurable lesson, "don't you see, my dear boy, that I'm teaching the whole thing in one fell swoop. That's the trinity I'm demonstrating in today's lesson. Another six or seven lessons and you'll be as learned as any doctor at the Sorbonne!"

YOUR WISH IS MY COMMAND or AS YOU LIKE IT

*M*y dear daughter," said the Baroness de Fréval to her eldest daughter, who was due to be married the following day, "you're as pretty as a picture, but the fact is you've barely turned thirteen. Still, no one is brighter or more attractive than you. Actually, I sometimes have the impression that your features were drawn by love itself, and yet here you are obliged to marry an elderly gentleman of the robe, whose idiosyncratic tastes are more than suspect . . . I'm most displeased by this mismatch, but your father insists on it. I wanted you to marry a man of rank, but such is not to be. I fear you are destined to spend your life bearing the burdensome title of *'présidente'*—a judge's wife.

"What upsets me even more is the notion that you may never be more than half a wife . . . modesty prevents me from explaining what I mean in graphic detail, my girl, but what I'm trying to say is that these foolish old rogues, who spend their lives passing judgment on others while carefully refraining from judging themselves, all have bizarre fantasies, used as they are to living a life of indolence. These dirty old men are born corrupt, they revel in dissolution, wallow in the slough of vice, and, crawling along in the muck both of the Justinian laws and the obscenities of the capital, remind one of the common garter snake that lifts its head from time to time to snag an insect. Like those indolent snakes, these foul creatures only emerge now and again to lodge some complaint or make an arrest . . .

"So listen to me carefully, young lady, and stand up straight . . . for if you tilt your head in that coquettish way, I'm sure the judge will find it totally seductive and, I have no doubt, try to back you into a corner then and there. In short, my child, here is what I am trying to say: whatever your husband first asks you to do, turn him down cold. We're as sure as we can be that the first thing he will ask of you will be as indecent as it is bizarre . . . We know his tastes like the back of our hand, for forty-five years now it's been common knowledge that, in keeping with principles that are completely ridiculous, this wicked old double-dealing knave has a decided preference for the rear door. Therefore, my child, you are to say 'no' to his first request, and I want to make it very clear that when he asks you should respond to him in the following way:

"'No, Monsieur, anywhere else you like, but most assuredly not *there!*'"

Having spoken her piece, the baroness had her daughter bathed, perfumed, and dressed in her finest robe. The judge arrived, his hair all in curls like those of the latest doll, powdered from head to shoulders, talking for all he was worth in a voice as shrill as it was nasal, citing this law and that and spouting statutory rules and regulations galore. From the cut of his tight-fitting clothes, his fashionable wig, and his fat pudgy fingers, he could have passed for a man of forty, though in fact he was nearing sixty. The bride-to-be appeared, he paraded around like the cock of the walk, and it was clear from the glint in his eyes the depths of depravity that lay in his heart.

The following day, the ceremony joining these two unlikely persons together having been performed, they repaired to the bridal chamber. They both disrobed and climbed into bed. And for the first time in his life the judge, either because he decided he should make haste slowly and take the time to educate his young pupil or because he was afraid of the possible sarcastic remarks his young bride might make if he were to make untoward demands upon her that first night, had resigned himself to culling naught but legitimate pleasures. But Mademoiselle de Fréval, who had paid the strictest attention to her mother's admonitions, and remembering clearly her sound advice that she should refuse whatever her husband's initial request might be, did exactly as she had been told. So as they lay in close embrace and the old judge began to make his intentions clear, she protested:

"No, Monsieur, under no circumstances will I consent to your doing *that*. Anywhere else you like, but most certainly not *there!*"

"Madame," the judge retorted, completely taken aback, "I assure you . . . I take full responsibility . . . if you must know, what I'm suggesting comes as a result of a great deal of self-control on my part . . . in fact, I might term it an act of virtue."

"No, Monsieur, you can try as long and as hard as

you like to talk me into doing that, but the answer is still no. And always will be."

"Well, in that case, Madame, I'll have to do my best to please you. As they say, your wish is my command," sighed the elderly judge. And seizing that part of her anatomy he loved most dearly he went on: "The last thing in the world I want to do is displease you, especially on our wedding night, but you should be well aware, Madame, that in the future, no matter how hard you try to make me change my course, I shall always refuse to say no."

"That's fine with me," said the young girl, "and you need have no fear that I shall ever ask you to change your ways."

"All right, then," he said resignedly, and following in the well-worn footsteps of Ganymede and Socrates, he murmured, "as you like it."

AN EYE FOR AN EYE

A solid, upstanding bourgeois, a native of Picardy who may well have been a descendant of one of those illustrious troubadours who dwelt along the banks of the Oise and Somme rivers some centuries back and who, a scant ten or twelve years ago, had been dragged back out of oblivion by one of this era's great writers,[1] this good and decent bourgeois, as I was saying, lived in the city of St. Quentin, renowned for the many famous men it has given to Literature.[2] He lived there with his wife and a female third cousin, the latter a nun in a local convent. This third cousin was a small, dark-haired young lass, with a mischievous face, flashing eyes, a turned-up nose, and a trim little figure. She was twenty-two years old and had been a nun for four. Sister Petronille—for that was her name—had a lovely voice and a temperament more inclined toward the profane than the sacred.

As for our Monsieur d'Escaloponville, for such was the name of our worthy bourgeois, he was a stout, good-natured fellow of twenty-eight, who happened to find his cousin far more enticing than Madame d'Escaloponville, with whom he had been sharing a bed for ten years, and as is well-known such a ten-year habit is bound to douse the fires lit by Hymen.

Madame d'Escaloponville—for it is our bounden duty to depict her, what would they think of us if we failed to give you an accurate portrait in an age when portraits are all the rage, when even a tragic play would be turned down for performance if it did not contain at least six subjects the merchants could seize upon and exploit[3]—Madame d'Escaloponville, I repeat, was a slightly lusterless blonde, with a porcelain skin, pretty eyes, on the plumpish side, and the kind of well-filled-out cheeks that lead people to comment on "how good you look."

Up till now, Madame d'Escaloponville had been completely unaware that there is a way to take revenge on an unfaithful husband. As virtuous as her mother had been before her—and that dear lady had lived with the same man for eighty-three years without ever being unfaithful to him[4]—she was still naive enough, still innocent enough in the ways of the world, not to have even the slightest suspicion of this crime that the casuists have dubbed "adultery" and those of a less rigorous nature, who filter everything through a softer lens, simply refer to as "dalliance." But the resentment that a woman betrayed feels soon cries out for revenge, and since no one likes to be accused of being negligent, there is nothing in her power she won't do to exact her revenge in such a way that she will be viewed as blameless.

Finally, Madame d'Escaloponville's eyes were opened to the fact that her dear husband was spending more time with his third cousin, at which point her heart and soul were in thrall to the green-eyed monster, jealousy. She spied on him, made inquiries, and before long discovered what everyone else in St. Quentin seemed to know, namely that her husband and Sister Petronille were having an affair. Feeling herself now on solid ground, Madame d'Escaloponville duly informed her husband that his untoward behavior was more painful to her than she could say, adding that her own conduct did not warrant such treatment, and begged him to mend his wicked ways.

"My wicked ways?" he responded matter-of-factly. "Are you unaware that by sleeping with my cousin the nun I am helping to save my soul? Such a holy affair cleanses one's soul, brings one closer to the Supreme Being, makes us one with the Holy Ghost. With people who have given themselves to God, my dear wife, there can be no sin. Everything one does with them purifies, opens one to the path of heavenly bliss."

Madame d'Escaloponville, more than slightly unhappy at her lack of success in confronting her husband, said nothing, but in her heart of hearts vowed that she would find some way to seek revenge that was as convincing as it was irreproachable. The devilish thing about such decisions is that women can somehow always find a way: even if they are not overly attractive, they have but to snap their fingers and avengers flood in on all sides.

In this same town there was a certain curate of the parish, a man named Abbé du Bosquet, a tall man, about thirty, of decidedly lecherous tendencies, who had hotly pursued every woman in town and caused a veritable forest of horns to sprout upon the brows of St. Quentin's husbands. Madame d'Escaloponville introduced herself to the curate. Little by little the curate got to know

Madame d'Escaloponville better, until there came a point when it is safe to say that they knew each other so perfectly that each could have painted a full-length portrait of the other in such intimate detail that anyone viewing them would have identified them immediately.

At the end of a month, people began congratulating poor Monsieur d'Escaloponville, who till then had been wont to claim that he and he alone had escaped the curate's formidable amorous assaults, and he and he alone in all of St. Quentin had the good fortune of not having his brow sullied by the scoundrel's exploits.

"That surely can't be," said d'Escaloponville to one of those who had come to speak to him about the matter. "My wife is as chaste as Lucretia.[5] I don't care if you tell me the same thing a hundred times over, I still won't believe it."

"Seeing's believing," said the friend. "Come and see for yourself. And then we'll talk about doubts."

D'Escaloponville reluctantly agreed to follow his friend, who led him to a place about half a league out of town, a secluded spot where the Somme River, flanked on both banks by newly flowering hedgerows, forms a lovely pool where the townspeople were in the habit of coming to bathe. But since the hour when the two lovers had agreed to meet was earlier than the time people came to bathe, our poor husband had the misfortune of seeing first his honest wife then his rival, without anyone there to disturb them.

"What do you say?" d'Escaloponville's friend whispered. "Your forehead beginning to itch?"

"Not yet," the lady's husband responded, nonetheless letting his hand stray to his brow to check it out, "maybe she's come here to say confession."

"In that case, I suggest we stay to the bitter end."

They did not have long to wait. Scarcely had the two arrived in the shade of the sweet-smelling hedges than Abbé du Bosquet set about removing everything that stood in the way of the voluptuous fondling he had in mind, whereupon he proceeded, perhaps for the thirtieth time that month, to relegate piously good, honest d'Escaloponville to the ranks of the town's other husbands.

"Well," his friend said, "*now* do you believe?"

"Let's get out of here," d'Escaloponville said bitterly. "Not only do I believe, but I'm so convinced I wouldn't mind killing this vile priest. The only problem is, if I did the price I'd have to pay would be far more than he's worth. Let's go, my friend. And remember: mum's the word, I beg of you."

D'Escaloponville returned home upset and perplexed, and shortly thereafter his wife appeared and sat down to supper at his chaste side.

"Just a moment there, my pretty one," her husband said, in a state of rage. "Since I was a child I swore to my father I'd never dine with whores."

"With whores?" Madame d'Escaloponville replied with an air of innocence. "I'm surprised by your words, dear friend. Could you tell me what you blame me for?"

"What?" he sputtered. "What do I blame you for? Why, for doing what you did with our curate this afternoon at the bathing spot, that's what!"

"Oh, Good Lord!" the sweet woman replied. "Is

that all? Is that all you have to say to me, my good fellow?"

"Good God, what do you mean, 'is that all?'" d'Escaloponville managed.

"But my friend, all I did was follow your good advice. Didn't you tell me there was nothing wrong in sleeping with a member of the clergy, that such a holy affair had the virtue of cleansing one's soul, that it brought a person closer to the Supreme Being, that in so doing one was made flesh with the Holy Ghost; in short, that it opened the path to heavenly grace? And so, my friend, all I have done is what you told me to do, and far from being a whore I consider myself a saint! And I'll say this: if any one of those men of God has the means of finding, as you yourself put it, the path to heavenly grace, I assure you it's our curate, for I swear I've never seen a bigger key!"

THE WINDBAGS OF
PROVENCE

*D*uring the reign of Louis XIV an ambassador to
France from Persia appeared on the scene, as
everyone knows.[1] The Sun King loved to entice to his
court foreigners from every nation on the face of the
earth, who would be so impressed by the court's incom-
parable glitter they would return home bearing a few
beams from those glorious rays that covered the earth
from one end to the other.

The ambassador duly landed in Marseilles, where
the city fathers greeted him with great pomp and circumstance. Hearing which, the gentleman judges of the city
of Aix-en-Provence resolved not to be outdone when the
ambassador paid a visit to their city by a place which, in
their erroneous estimation, was far less important than
their own.

As a result, they set as the first of their many projects
a welcome speech delivered directly in Persian. It would
have been simple to greet him in Provençal, but the ambassador would not have understood a single word. This
weighty problem gave them great pause. The City
Council sat in grave deliberation—it must be said that it
has never taken very much for that august body to find

an excuse to deliberate: a dispute between peasants, some fuss or other about the local theater, and above all any case involving whores[2]—all these subjects are so much grist to these judges' mills, for indeed they have been an indolent lot ever since the time of François I, when they put the region to fire and sword, then watered it with the blood of the unfortunate people who dwelt there.[3]

Thus did they deliberate in plenary session. But no matter how long and hard they discussed the matter, they simply could not come up with a solution to the burning question: how could they find a way of delivering the welcoming speech in Persian? Was it even possible, in that Society of Fishmongers, who just happened to be garbed in judicial black robes, that one of them could speak Persian (especially considering that not a man amongst them could even speak proper French)?

Nonetheless, the speech was written: three famous lawyers had labored over it for six weeks. Finally, either from within their own ranks or somewhere in the town of Aix, they tracked down a sailor who had lived for several years in the Near East and who spoke Persian almost as fluently as he spoke his native tongue. He was duly informed about what was expected of him, and accepted to play the role. He learned the speech by heart and translated it into Persian without a hitch.

When the appointed day arrived, they clothed him in the black cassock of a high court judge, loaned him the most august wig of the entire magistrates' court, and followed by the entire corps of judges he made his way toward the ambassador. They had rehearsed to the letter the roles each should play, and the orator had stressed to

those personages in his wake that they should keep their
eyes glued upon him and, no matter what, emulate his
every move, without fail.

The ambassador advanced to the center of the courtyard where, he had been instructed, he would be greeted
by the welcoming committee. The sailor made a deep
bow, and, unaccustomed as he was to wearing a wig, at
the nadir of his bow it fell and landed at the ambassador's
feet. The retinue of members of the bench, who had
promised to imitate the sailor's every move, promptly
bowed just as deeply and also shed their respective wigs,
casting them at the ambassador's feet, thus exposing
their bald, and in some cases quite mangy, heads. Non-
plussed, the sailor plucked his wig from the floor, put it
back on his head, and, in ringing tones, began to deliver
the welcoming speech, in such excellent Persian that the
ambassador was sure the orator was one of his country-
men. The very thought sent him into a rage.

"Miserable creature!" he shouted, putting his hand
threateningly on his sword. "There's no way you could
speak my native tongue so fluently unless you are a rene-
gade, someone who has renounced his religion and
turned his back on the Prophet. Infidel! you must pay for
your sins. Off with your head!"

The poor sailor did his best to defend himself, to no
avail. He waved his arms up and down and from side to
side; he swore up a storm till he was blue in the face. All
of which the Areopagitic[4] troupe behind him energeti-
cally emulated to the letter, gesture for gesture, word for
word. Finally, not knowing how else to extricate himself
from this pretty pickle, he thought of a stratagem that he
deemed would be irrefutable, namely to unbutton his

trousers and produce for the ambassador proof positive that he never in his life had been circumcised. This latest gesture on his part was immediately emulated by the full magisterial troupe, as a result of which there were suddenly some forty or fifty Provençal judges with their flies open and foreskins in hand, proving, as had the sailor before them, that there was not one amongst them who was any less Christian than Saint Christopher himself. It is not difficult to imagine that the ladies viewing the ceremony from their windows above were highly amused by the pantomime taking place below.

Finally, the ambassador, convinced by such irrefutable evidence, realized that the orator was guiltless and that, for better or worse, he had landed in what, in his mind, he dubbed "The City of Trousers."

He also decided not to make any further issue, shrugged, and said (doubtless to himself): "I'm not surprised that people such as these keep a gallows always at the ready, for closed minds, which are the other side of the coin of incompetence, must be the basic characteristic of these barely human creatures."

News of the event having been bruited abroad, it was thought that this new manner of proclaiming one's faith should be immortalized, and in fact a young painter who had been present at the spectacle had already made some preliminary sketches from life. But the court banned the work, consigned it to flames, and banished the painter from the province. In doing so it never even crossed their minds they were burning themselves, since they were all very clearly portrayed in the sketches.

"We don't mind being taken for imbeciles," the judges said in all seriousness. "Even if we did, it wouldn't matter, for we have made fools of ourselves for a very long time now, as anyone in France can attest. What we do mind, however, is a painting depicting our stupidity for future generations. Posterity will soon forget this little incident, and will remember it no more than it does Mérindol and Cabrières.[5] For the honor of the bench, 'tis much better to be murderers than to be remembered as asses."

ROOM FOR TWO

*T*here lived on the rue Saint-Honoré in Paris the very pretty wife of a bourgeois, a young woman of twenty-two. Slightly on the plump side, her body was nonetheless as charming as it was appetizing, though as I said a tad generous in its contours. In addition to all these charms, she was possessed of a divine bosom, and to these physical attributes was joined a quick wit, vivaciousness, and a most lively taste for all the worldly pleasures that are forbidden by the strict rules of marriage. Roughly a year earlier, she had made up her mind to hire two assistants for her husband, who, being both ugly and old, not only displeased her greatly but acquitted himself of his husbandly duties only rarely, and when he did he performed them poorly. In fact, had he fulfilled them a trifle better, chances are he would have appeased his demanding wife, Dolmene, for such was our pretty young lady's name.

The arrangements she made with her two lovers could not have been better: Des-Roues, a young army officer, came from four to five in the afternoon, following which a young businessman named Dolbreuse, who was uncommonly handsome, came between five-thirty and seven. These were the best times she could manage, for only during these hours was she sure not to be disturbed. Mornings she had to spend at the shop, and sometimes in the evening as well, or else her husband might show up and she would be compelled to discuss business matters with him. Moreover, Madame Dolmene had confided to one of her women friends that she rather liked having these affairs follow hard upon each other. That way, the fires of the imagination were still burning bright, she opined, and nothing was more pleasant than going from one pleasure to another without having to stoke the furnace afresh. For Madame Dolmene was a charming creature who knew how to calculate to perfection the various feelings and emotions of love. Few women were more talented than she in analyzing these nuances, from which she had determined that when all was said and done, two lovers were far better than one. As far as one's reputation was concerned, it was more or less the same thing: one lover covered for the other, so to speak, and anyone who happened to notice could easily have mistaken the second lover for the first: they might think it was one person coming and going several times a day. And yet as far as the pleasure derived, what a difference! There was also another factor: Madame Dolmene was terribly afraid of getting pregnant, and knowing that her husband would never commit the folly of ruining her waistline, had also reasoned that with two lovers there was much less risk of what she dreaded on that score than there was with one because, as she put it, good anatomist that she was, the two fruits of love would mutually destroy each other.

One day, the strictly established order of these two assignations got slightly mixed up, and as we shall see, the two lovers, who had never met, made each other's acquaintance in a rather unusual albeit pleasant way. Des-Roues, lover number one, arrived a trifle behind schedule and, as if the Devil himself had had a hand in it, Dolbreuse, lover number two, happened to arrive a bit early.

The discerning reader will readily see that the combination of these two seemingly innocuous mistakes unfortunately had to lead inevitably to an encounter: and so it did. But let us try to describe just what took place with all the modesty and restraint we can muster in a situation that in itself is extremely licentious.

Through a strange quirk of fate—but then again, is life not filled with them?—our young army officer, a bit weary of playing the role of lover, wanted for a moment to play that of mistress. Instead of being held in the arms of his beloved, he wanted to hold her differently; in a word, what was down he turned up, and by this reversal of roles Madame Dolmene, naked as the Venus of Callipygus,[1] bending over the altar of love upon which the sacrifice is usually performed, was astride her lover, thus presenting to the door of the bedroom, where these ritual mysteries were being celebrated, that part of the body the Greeks worship with such devotion, portrayed so eloquently in the above-named statue, that part of the body which is undeniably lovely and to which, without looking very hard, one can find so many adoring adepts in Paris itself. Such was the position of our lovers when Dolbreuse, who had the run of the house, arrived humming a merry tune under his breath and cast his eyes on the anatomy that any decent and proper woman is never supposed to show.

What might well have been a source of unmitigated pleasure to so many people made Dolbreuse stop in his tracks.

"What's this I see?" he cried out. "You traitor! Is·this what you have in store for me?"

Madame Dolmene, who at that very moment was experiencing one of those crises during which a woman's body is far more in charge of her being than is her mind, resolved to pay him back in kind.

"What the devil's your problem?" she said to the second Adonis, without ceasing to give herself totally to the first. "I don't see anything in all this that should upset you so. Don't let us disturb you, my friend. Come, join in the fun: as you can see, there's plenty of room for two."

Dolbreuse, who couldn't refrain from laughing at his mistress's sangfroid, decided that the best thing would be to follow her good advice without further ado and join in the fun.

From all reports, all three had a rollicking good time.

THE HUSBAND WHO
TURNED PRIEST:
A TALE OF PROVENCE

*I*n Provence, between the towns of Menerbe and Apt,[1] in the county of Avignon, there stands a small, isolated convent called Saint-Hilaire, which is perched on the side of a hill so steep that even goats have trouble grazing there.[2] This modest place serves more or less as a cesspool for all the surrounding Carmelite communities, a place to which those in its ranks who have in any way dishonored the order are summarily dispatched. Thus it is easy to imagine the pristine nature of the convent's inhabitants: drunkards, womanizers, sodomites, and gamblers—such is the noble composition of the place: recluses who in this scandal-ridden retreat offer to God, as best they can, the hearts on which the rest of the world has turned its back. As neighbors there were but few: a château or two[3] and, a scant league from the convent, the town of Menerbe itself—such were the entire surroundings of these good clerics who, despite their cassocks and their calling, did not always find their neighbors' doors open to them.

For some time now, Father Gabriel, one of the saints

of this hermitage, had his eye on a certain woman of Menerbe whose husband, Monsieur Rodin, was, if ever there was one, a born cuckold. Madame Rodin was a petite brunette of twenty-eight, with a mischievous pair of eyes and perfectly rounded buttocks; in short, a mouth-watering dish to set before a monk. As for Monsieur Rodin, he was a decent enough fellow, going quietly about his business. He had sold cloth for a living and at one point had been a town provost.* In other words, what is commonly known as an honest burgher. Though not totally sure of the tender virtue of his better half, he was nonetheless enough of a philosopher to understand that the best way of preventing an excessive growth of horns on one's forehead was simply to pretend they weren't there. In his earlier days, he had studied for the priesthood. He spoke Latin as well as Cicero himself, and often enjoyed playing checkers with Father Gabriel, who, sly and clever lover-to-be that he was, knew that if it was the wife you were after, you should always insinuate yourself to some degree into the husband's good graces. Among the sons of Elijah,[4] Father Gabriel was a real stud. Looking at him, one had the impression that, if necessary, the task of repopulating the entire earth could be left entirely in his capable hands. If ever there was a begetter of children, it was Gabriel. He stood six feet tall and, it was said, was as well endowed as any mule in the region (a specialty, so we are told, of the Carmelite fathers); a swarthy fellow with eyebrows that would have

---

*A municipal employee roughly the equivalent of a bailiff.

put Jupiter to shame, he was possessed of a solid pair of shoulders, and a back as broad as the trunk of an alder. What woman would not have been irresistibly drawn to such a strapping, bawdy fellow? And it must be confessed that Madame Rodin did find him astonishingly seductive, endowed as he clearly was with attributes she had found sorely lacking in the decent lord and master her parents had chosen for her. As we have said, Monsieur Rodin appeared to close his eyes to everything, but that did not mean he wasn't jealous. He did not say a word, but he was always there, including times he clearly should have been elsewhere. And yet the pear was ripe for plucking. In fact, the naive Madame Rodin had quite openly declared to her would-be lover that all she was waiting for to respond to his desires—which seemed far too ardent to resist any longer—was the proper occasion. And on his end, Father Gabriel made it known that he was ready and willing, and certainly able ... In a very brief moment when Monsieur Rodin had been obliged to step out, Father Gabriel had flashed before his charming mistress's eyes credentials that help a woman—assuming she is still on the fence—make up her mind once and for all.

One day Rodin had invited himself to lunch with Father Gabriel at Saint-Hilaire, suggesting that after lunch they go hunting together. After they had downed a few good bottles of Lanerte[5] wine, Father Gabriel thought that fate had finally handed him on a silver platter the occasion he had been waiting for.

"Oh, Good God, my dear provost," said the monk to his friend, "you don't know how glad I am to see you.

You couldn't have come at a better time. I have a very urgent business matter to attend to, and you can be of great service to me."

"What's the business matter, Father?"

"Do you know a man in Menerbe named Renoult?"

"Renoult the hatmaker?"

"That's the one."

"So . . . ?"

"Well, this wily rascal owes me a hundred *écus*, and I've just heard a while ago that he's on the verge of going under. In fact, he may well be on his way out of the county as we speak. It's absolutely imperative that I go see him this minute."

"So what's stopping you?"

"My mass, damn it, my mass. I have to say mass. Oh! if only I could say the hell with mass and have the hundred *écus* securely in my pocket . . ."

"Do you mean to say you can't find someone to say mass for you?"

"Oh, spare me. There are only three of us here, and if we don't say mass three times a day the Father Superior, who never says it himself, will report us to Rome. But there is a way you can help, my friend, if only you're willing. It's all in your hands."

"Good God, of course I'm only too willing to help. What do I have to do?"

"I'm here alone with the sexton. The two earlier masses have already been said, and both the other monks are off the premises somewhere. No one will be any the wiser. It will be an insignificant congregation, no more than a handful of peasants and that devout little lady from the Château de ***, who lives a half league from here, an angelic creature who thinks that by being devout she can atone for her husband's escapades.[6] You once told me you had studied for the priesthood, isn't that so?"

"Indeed I did."

"So you must have learned how to say mass."

"As well as the archbishop himself!"

"Oh, my dear, good friend!" Father Gabriel went on, pulling Rodin to him in a bear hug, "for God's sake, put on these robes. It's ten o'clock now. At the stroke of eleven, say the mass, I beg of you. Our brother the sexton is a good fellow; he won't ever betray us. If anyone in the congregation happens to notice it's not me, we'll tell him it's a new monk, and those who don't notice can stew in their ignorance.

"I'm going to hie off to see this rogue of a hatmaker, and either I'll have my money or he'll pay with his life. I'll be back in no more than two hours. Hold lunch for me; after mass, grill us a sole, fry up some eggs, open the wine. As soon as I'm back we'll eat lunch, then off we'll go hunting . . . Yes, my friend, a-hunting we will go. And I have a strong feeling that today's hunt will be most excellent. In fact, I've heard tell that some horned beast has recently been seen in these parts. By God! We'll bag him for sure, even if it brings twenty lawsuits down on our heads from the lord of the manor."[7]

"It seems like a good plan," Rodin said, "and as a favor I'm prepared to do it. In fact, there's almost nothing I wouldn't do for you, Father. But tell me: wouldn't I be committing a sin?"

"A sin, my friend? Not at all. There might be if a priest botched a mass, but as for the words said by someone who is not ordained, it's the same as if the words had not been uttered at all. Believe me, I'm a casuist, and there is nothing in all this that would qualify as a venial sin."

"But do I have to say the words?"

"And why not? These words are meaningful only in our mouths. The power is vested in us, not in the words themselves. You see, all I'd have to do is pronounce these words over your wife's belly for me to metamorphose the temple wherein you make your sacrifice into the body of Christ... No, no, my friend, we and we alone have the power of transubstantiation. You, Rodin, can utter the words twenty thousand times over without the Holy Spirit ever once descending. Even with us it sometimes fails completely. It's all a matter of faith. In the words of Jesus Christ, with a bit of faith no bigger than the size of a grain of sand, one can move mountains, you know. Take me, for example: sometimes when I'm saying mass my mind wanders and I find myself thinking about the girls and women in the congregation, not about the damn little wafer I'm holding in my fingers. Do you think that in such cases I can get anything to descend? I'd be better off believing in the Koran than in stuffing my head with that sort of twaddle. In any event, your mass will for all intents and purposes be just as good as mine. So don't give it another thought! Everything will go just fine!"

"Good God above!" Rodin exclaimed. "I'm starved! And still two hours to go before lunch."

"So what's to keep you from having a bite right now? Here: there's plenty more where that came from."

"And what about the mass I'm supposed to say?"

"Eh? Good Lord, what difference does that make? Do you think it makes any difference to Him whether He lands in a full stomach rather than an empty one? Whether the wafer lies on top of or underneath the rest of the food? I'll be damned if it makes the slightest difference, at least in my opinion. Come, come, my friend, if I had to go to Rome every time I've eaten before I said mass, I'd be constantly on the road. Anyway, as I said, you're not a priest, so you're not bound by the rules. You're only to give an *image* of the mass, not the real thing. So you can do whatever you like before or after— even screw your wife if she was here. All you have to do is emulate me. You're not really celebrating mass or consummating the sacrifice."

"In that case by all means," said Rodin. "Full speed ahead, and don't give it another thought!"

"Good," said Father Gabriel, rushing out the door, leaving his friend in the good hands of the sexton. "You can count on me, my friend, I'll be back inside two hours and then I'm all yours!"

And with that the monk hurried on his way, pleased as punch with his little scheme.

One can imagine that he wasted no time arriving at the doorstep of the provost's wife. Surprised to see him, and thinking he was supposed to be with her husband, she asked him what the reason was for such an unexpected visit.

"Let's not waste precious minutes, my sweet," said the monk, who was quite out of breath. "We don't have very much time. First a glass of wine, then let's to it without further ado."

"But what about my husband?"

"He's saying mass."

"Saying *mass?*"

"You heard me, my love, saying mass," said the Carmelite as he tumbled the dear lady head over heels onto the bed. "'Tis true, my love, I've turned your husband into a priest, and while he is celebrating a divine mystery, let us hasten to celebrate a secular one."

The monk was, as noted, a sturdy fellow, and when he had hold of a woman it was hard to resist him. Moreover, his reasoning was so conclusive that he quickly won her over. Nor did he find it all that difficult to persuade a hot-blooded Provençal woman of twenty-two[8] summers, so much in fact that he convinced her a second time.

"Oh, you angel sent from heaven," she said at long last, now thoroughly won over, "do you know what time it is? We must take our leave. If our pleasures are limited to the length of the mass then he must already have reached the *missa est.*"

"No, no, my dove," said the Carmelite, armed and ready with a further argument to offer Madame Rodin, "don't give it another thought, my pet, we have all the time in the world. Let's have another go, my dear. These novices up there don't go as fast as we. One more time, what do you say? I'll bet your cuckold of a husband hasn't even got to the part where the wafer is raised aloft."

But leave each other they finally did, not without promising however to see each other again and not without discussing a number of ways and means to make that happen. After which Gabriel rejoined Rodin.

The good fellow had celebrated the mass as flawlessly as any bishop.

"The only problem I ran into," he said proudly, was

the *quod aures*, which I flubbed slightly. At that juncture I was supposed to drink but instead I began to eat. But the sexton straightened me out.... And what about your hundred *écus*, Father?"

"I got them all right. The rascal tried to worm his way out of it, but I grabbed a pitchfork and, by God, gave him a sound thrashing—on his head, all over."

Once the meal was over, our two friends went out hunting as they had planned. When he got home, Rodin told his wife about the favor he had just done for Father Gabriel.

"I celebrated mass," the stupid ninny bragged, laughing wholeheartedly. "Yes, by God, I celebrated mass like a real priest while Father Gabriel was out giving a sound thrashing to that rascal Renoult. Browbeat the man, that's what he did, my pet, what do you think of that? Raised welts on his head and shoulders, he told me. I bet those welts on his forehead are by now the size of goose eggs, my love. What a funny story that is, don't you find? I tell you, those with bumps on their heads make me laugh! ... And what about you, my sweet, what were you up to while I was saying mass?"

"Ah! my friend," the provost's wife replied, "it would seem that both of us were inspired by heaven today. We were both filled with celestial elements and neither one of us knew it! While you were saying mass, I was reciting that lovely prayer the Virgin gave to the angel Gabriel when he appeared unto her and told her she would be with child through the intervention of the Holy Ghost. Oh, my friend, we are on the road to salvation, of that I am sure, and will remain there just so long as both of us keep on performing such good works."

THIEVES AND SWINDLERS

*A*s far back as anyone can remember, there has been in Paris a class of men who insinuate themselves into all segments of society and whose sole profession is to live off others. Nothing is more clever or more cunning than the various and sundry schemes of these evil men and women, who, one way or another, will go to any lengths to snare innocent victims in their nets. While the main body of this army works in the city itself, various detachments flutter about on the outskirts, scattered about throughout the length and breadth of the countryside, generally traveling from one place to another by public coach.

These grim but undeniably accurate facts having been established, let us now turn our attention to the naive young lady who it will sadden us to the point of tears to see fall into the hands of such ignominious people.

Rosette de Farville, the daughter of a solid bourgeois from the city of Rouen in western France, had nagged her father so long and so insistently that he had finally relented and given her permission to go to Paris at Carnival time[1] and stay with her uncle Mathieu, a wealthy money-lender who lived on the rue Quincampoix.[2]

Though more than a trifle naive, Rosette, who was well into her nineteenth year, was as pretty as a picture, with blond hair and lovely blue eyes, skin that was dazzlingly white, and a bosom that, though concealed beneath a light layer of gauze, promised to anyone with practiced eyes that what remained hidden from view was at least the equal of what one could discern.

The parting of father and daughter was tearful; it was the first time his daughter had left the paternal nest. She was a good girl, she was fully capable of looking out for herself, she was staying with a kindly relative, she would be back in time before Easter: all these arguments were reassuring to her father. But on the other hand, Rosette was extremely pretty. Rosette was a trusting soul, and she was going to a city known to be dangerous for any of the fair sex from the provinces who landed there full of innocence and a goodly portion of virtue.

Still in all, the girl set off, taking with her a wardrobe that would enable her to cut a fine figure in Paris in her modest circle, not to mention a considerable quantity of jewelry and presents not only for her Uncle Mathieu himself but also for his daughters, her cousins Adelaide and Sophie. Her father embraced her, bade her a fond farewell, and asked the coachman to keep an eye on her throughout the trip. The driver cracked his whip; tears were shed on both sides as the coach drove off. But it must be said that a father's tender feelings for his children are stronger and deeper than the reverse. Nature is such that it allows young offspring to discover pleasures that turn their heads, various social diversions that, without meaning to, distance them from their parents and, in their hearts, chill those feelings of tenderness that, for both parents, is more focused, more ardent, and far more sincere. Parents are well aware of this fatal indifference on the part of their children who, turning their backs on the pleasurable experiences of their youth, can come to look upon their parents as no more or no less than the sacred vessels to whom they owe their existence.

Rosette was no exception to that general rule of Nature, and her tears were soon dry as her thoughts focused on the pleasures that awaited her in Paris. She wasted no time in introducing herself to the other passengers who were headed there and who, she assumed, knew the city far better than she. Her first question was to find out in what part of Paris the rue Quincampoix was located.

"Why, that's in my part of town," said a tall, well-built fellow who, because of the kind of uniform he was wearing and his imposing tone of voice, had been dominating the conversation in the carriage as it jolted along.

"What, Monsieur, you mean to say you actually *live* on the rue Quincampoix?"

"I do, and have for some twenty years now."

"Oh! Then you must know my Uncle Mathieu."

"Monsieur Mathieu is your *uncle*, Mademoiselle?"

"Yes, indeed. I'm his niece, and I'm on my way to see him. I'm going to spend the rest of the winter with him and my two cousins, Adelaide and Sophie, whom I'm sure you know as well."

"Of course I know them! In fact, Monsieur Mathieu is my next-door neighbor and, it just so happens, I've been in love with one of his daughters these past five years."

"You're in love with one of my cousins! I'll bet it's Sophie."

"No, as a matter of fact it's Adelaide. Have you ever seen a more beautiful face in your life?"

"That's what everybody in Rouen says . . . I can't say for myself, I must confess, for I've never actually seen them myself. This is my first visit to the capital."

"Ah, so you don't know your cousins, eh? And I bet you've never laid eyes on your uncle either?"

"Good lord no! He left Rouen the same year I was born and never came back."

"He's a very proper gentleman, I can assure you of that, and he'll be delighted to have you."

"It's a lovely house, I understand."

"It is indeed, though he rents out part of it. He only keeps the apartment on the second floor for himself."

"And the ground floor too, I think."

"Quite right. And as I understand it, one room on the top floor as well."

"Oh, I know he's quite a wealthy man, but I assure you I won't disgrace him while I'm under his roof. Look: here's a hundred double *louis* my father gave me to buy clothes with, so that I'll be as fashionable as any young lady in town and my cousins won't ever be ashamed of me. And look at these earrings I'm bringing for my cousin Adelaide—the sister you're in love with. They're worth at least a hundred *louis*. And this necklace I'm bringing as a present to Sophie: it's worth just as much as the earrings. And that's not all: this little gold box, which contains a miniature portrait of my mother, was just yesterday valued at fifty *louis*. It's a present from my father to Uncle Mathieu. Taken all together, between the money and the jewels, plus my own clothes, I'm sure I have more than five hundred *louis'* worth with me."

"You needn't have gone to such lengths to be welcome at your Uncle Mathieu's," said the swindler, casting a greedy eye at the lovely young lady and her *louis*. "The mere presence of your company will mean far more to him, I'm sure, than all these little baubles."

"That may well be. Still in all, my father's a firm believer in doing things right, and he doesn't want anyone to look down their nose at us just because we're country folk."

"The truth is, Mademoiselle, you're such pleasant company that if I had my way I'd make you stay on in Paris and convince your uncle to have his son marry you."

"His son! He doesn't have a son."

"I mean his *nephew*. You know, the very tall young man . . ."

"Who, Charles?"

"That's the one, Charles! My closest friend, *parbleau!*"

"You mean you knew Charles, Monsieur?"

"Knew him is an understatement, Mademoiselle. Why, as I said he's my closest friend. Knew him, know him: in fact, he's the only reason I'm going to Paris."

"I'm afraid you're mistaken, Monsieur. Poor Charles is dead. From the time I was a little girl I was supposed to marry him. I never had the pleasure of meeting him, but I was always told he was a lovely man. Then he got it into his head to join the army, went off to war, and was killed."

"All well and good, Mademoiselle. I can see that my fondest wish is about to come true. They have a major surprise in store for you in Paris, Mademoiselle, of that you may be sure. Charles is not dead, as everyone thought. He came back six months ago, safe and sound. He wrote me and announced he was getting married. And that's doubtless why you're being sent to Paris. Four days from now you and Charles will be man and wife, and all those presents you're carrying are actually wedding presents."

"You know, Monsieur," Rosette replied, "what you're saying makes all sorts of sense. Putting your conjectures together with some remarks my father made these past few days, which now come back to me, I can see that everything you said is completely plausible. Just think: getting married in Paris! Oh, Monsieur, it gives me goose bumps! But if that happens, then you must marry cousin Adelaide without delay. I'll do my best to talk her into it. What a handsome foursome we'll make!"

Such was the tone and tenor of the conversation between the good, sweet Rosette and the no-good scoundrel who was sounding her out as the carriage rocked along and whose sole intent was to take full advantage of the poor inexperienced lass who had unburdened herself to him with total candor. What a rich haul for this band of libertines: five hundred *louis* and a pretty young girl to boot! Tell me in all truth, which of your senses would not be tickled by such an appealing prospect?

As they were nearing Pontoise,[3] the crook said:

"I have a great idea, Mademoiselle. I'll get out here, hire a horse, and dash off to your uncle's to announce your impending arrival. That way the whole family will come out to greet you, I'm sure, and you won't feel so alone or intimidated at arriving in this great city."

The plan is agreed to, the pseudo-gentleman hops

down, hires a horse, and races off to forewarn the actors he had chosen for his forthcoming play: he rehearses them as to their roles, and when they are ready two carriages bear the pseudo-family to Saint Denis,[4] where they repair to the local inn. When Rosette's carriage arrives, her former traveling companion, the head swindler, takes charge of the introductions: Uncle Mathieu, Charles, tall and impressive in his army uniform, and Rosette's two charming cousins.

Embraces are exchanged all around, the young Normandy lass delivers her father's letters, the good Monsieur Mathieu weeps tears of joy upon learning his brother is in good health. In Paris, Rosette is made to understand, one distributes presents as soon as one meets. In any event, Rosette, more than anxious to display the full extent of her father's generosity, hurriedly hands them over to each party in turn. Further embraces all around, more proffered thanks, after which the party proceeds to the scoundrel's headquarters, which they tell our unsuspecting beauty is on the rue Quincampoix. They arrive at a respectable enough house, Mademoiselle Farville is shown to her room, her trunk is brought up to her, and then they all announce they are famished and sit down at the table. As they dine, they make sure to serve Rosette more to drink than is good for her. Used as she is to drinking only cider, Rosette is easily persuaded that Champagne is made out of Paris apples and she happily drinks all they pour until she is high as a kite. Once she is utterly defenseless, they strip her stark naked and our band of lowlife scoundrels, assured now that she is bereft of all her possessions except those with which Nature had endowed her, desiring to leave not even these intact or unsullied, spend the entire night defiling them in one way or another to their heart's content.

Finally, pleased that they had got from the poor girl all that could be got, satisfied that they have stolen from her not only her reason but her honor and money as well, cover her with a tattered coat and, before the break of dawn, go and deposit her on the top steps of the Saint-Roche Church.[5]

Opening her eyes at the first light of dawn, the poor girl, more than upset by the appalling state in which she finds herself, gingerly feels herself all over, wondering whether she is in fact alive or dead. The local riffraff gather around her and for a long while make sport of her, but finally someone takes pity and responds to her request to be taken to the police station. There she relates her sad story, asks that they write to her father and that she be given shelter somewhere until he responds. The superintendent of police, seeing how frank and honest the girl's remarks are, takes her into his own home until her father arrives from Normandy. Generous tears are shed on both sides, after which he takes his darling daughter home, where she remains for the rest of her days, having not the slightest desire, it is said, ever to see the civilized capital of France again.

THE GASCON WIT

*A*n army officer from the region of Gascony[1] had, during the reign of Louis XIV, obtained from the king a special stipend of 150 *pistoles* for services rendered. With the royal order in hand, he barged into Monsieur Colbert's[2] quarters, without any advance warning, and found the minister dining with several other notables of the court.

"Which of you gentlemen," said the officer, in an accent that immediately betrayed his province of origin, "which of you, if you don't mind my asking, is Monsieur Colbert?"

"I am, good Sir," responded the minister. "How may I be of service to you?"

"A piddling matter, Monsieur, simply a bonus of 150 *pistoles* that I should like to have cashed forthwith."

Monsieur Colbert, who immediately realized that here was a fellow they might have some fun with, asked if he would mind too much if they finished their dinner, and, to temper the officer's impatience, invited him to join them at table.

"With great pleasure," replied the native of Gascony, "especially since I haven't yet had dinner."

Once the meal was over, the minister, who had

meanwhile sent up a note to the chief paymaster, told the officer that he could go upstairs to the office, where his money would be awaiting him. The soldier arrived, but the paymaster counted out only one hundred *pistoles.*

"Are you joking, Monsieur," he said to the clerk, "or are you blind? Can't you see that my requisition is for 150 *pistoles?*"

"Sir," the paymaster responded, "I can see very well that your requisition is for 150 *pistoles*, but I deducted fifty for the cost of your dinner with the minister."

"*Cadédis!*[3] Upon my word! Fifty *pistoles!* Why, at my inn they only charge me twenty *sous* for dinner."

"I'm sure they do. But there you don't have the distinct advantage of dining with the minister."

"You're right," said the Gascon. "That being the case, Monsieur, keep your money. Tell the minister that tomorrow evening I'll be back for dinner with one of my friends. That way we'll be even."

The Gascon's reply, and the practical joke that had occasioned it, made the rounds of the court the next day and was soon forgotten. They promptly added fifty *pistoles* to the officer's payout and sent him on his way. He went home to Gascony, where he sang the praises not only of Monsieur Colbert's dinner but indeed of the entire Versailles court, and especially the way they appreciated the sharp wit and spirit of the natives of Gascony.

And so I take my leave, Dear Reader. May health and happiness be yours, as our forefathers were wont to say after finishing their tale. Why not emulate their courtesy and candor? And so I shall say to you, Dear Reader, may good health, wealth, and pleasure be your lot. If my modest efforts have brought you a modicum of pleasure, then kindly give this volume a privileged spot on your bookshelf. And if I have bored you, then accept my sincere apologies and cast me into the fire without further ado.

NOTES

INTRODUCTION

1. Sade's wife, who was allowed to visit him in prison once a month, wrote in a letter dated May 25, 1787, that her husband was in fair health but growing "very fat," essentially because the authorities constantly denied him the right to daily walks to punish him for his recalcitrant acts or words.

2. Sade's father-in-law, Monsieur de Montreuil, had also been a chief judge of the Paris Cour des Aides, and one of his archrivals was the chief judge of the Paris Criminal Court, Judge Maupeou. Four years before Sade's sentence by the Aix court (that is, 1768), Maupeou was instrumental in having Sade arrested for another crime d'amour, the so-called Arcueil affair, and had personally signed the sentence committing him to prison for it. Again in Aix, Maupeou made his influence personally felt to strike a double blow: revenge against his hated rival, Sade's father-in-law, and against Sade himself, whom Maupeou rightly saw as an entrenched and unrepentant rebel against society and the state.

3. Sade served for several years in the army, rising to the rank of colonel and distinguishing himself in battle.

4. Sade, in a letter to his wife dated April 21, 1777 (that is, ten years before the composition of "The Mystified Magistrate"), makes the case that the prostitutes of Provence, or at least of Marseilles, "eat all sorts of unwholesome food every day of their lives," ergo suffer commonly from colic, ergo were not made ill by his "candied lozenges" but by their own gluttony.

5. A chief judge in France bears the title "President," and his wife therefore has the right to be called "Présidente." Sade's referral to Madame de Montreuil by that title was generally ironic, or disdainful.

6. On July 3, 1789, Sade, denied his daily walks on the Bastille ramparts because the reinforced garrison was becoming increasingly worried about the unrest in the streets below, retaliated by fashioning a makeshift megaphone, which he pushed through the bars of his cell, and shouting to the populace to come and save him and his fellow prisoners, whose throats "were being slit" (he was lying through his teeth).

7. Although he does not name him, Heine doubtless was referring first and foremost to Sade's younger son, Donatien-Claude-Armand, who immediately after his father's death in 1814 not only allowed but encouraged the authorities to burn his father's works, including the enormous *Days of Florbelle*, which Sade wrote between 1803 and 1807, during his final stay in Charenton.

8. It has been estimated that in the eighteenth century there were hundreds of brothels in France, catering to all tastes and classes. Police records also suggest that in Paris in the mid-1700s one out of seven women was a prostitute, and that statistic does not of course include the women of quality indulging in extramarital affairs, whose numbers, Sade maintains, were substantial.

9. Sade's nobility was of very old lineage, and through his mother, Marie-Eléonore de Maillé de Carman, he was directly allied to the Condé family, that is, to royal blood. His in-laws, the Montreuils, were of recent peerage—"new aristocrats"—and therefore especially sensitive to their position in the world.

10. Approximately three-fourths of Sade's writings were destroyed, some during his lifetime, many shortly after his death in 1814, some as recently as the 1940s, by the Nazi occupiers of France.

THE MYSTIFIED MAGISTRATE

1. Themis: In Greek mythology, the daughter of Uranus and Gaia, and the goddess of justice and law.

2. Jacques Cujas (1520–1590). A legal expert of the sixteenth century who adapted Roman—or Justinian—law to the needs of the time and the society where it was in use.

3. In the original Sade refers to d'Olincourt as "Count." In principle, in France a father bore the title of count and his son was a marquis. Upon his father's death in 1767, Sade in principle assumed the title "Count," and indeed signed documents as such. However, by this time his title and surname were so linked that, until the Revolution, he generally referred to himself as "Marquis." Here, for the sake of clarity and consistency, we shall refer to d'Olincourt as Marquis throughout.

4. Cumaean Sybil. In ancient Greece, Cumae was the site of the many prophetesses from whom one solicited advice and counsel, and through whom one asked favors of the gods. The Cumaean Sybil was the most famous of these prophetesses; it was she Aeneas consulted before descending to Avernus.

5. *parbleau.* An interjection, generally one of approval. The term is a corruption of *par Dieu*—by God.

6. The term that Sade uses in the original is *péchaire*, an interjection of endearment used in the South of France, especially in the Languedoc region.

7. Epidaurus. A town in Argolis, on the Aegean Sea, site of the Temple of Asclepius, to which thousands of Greeks of antiquity came to consult the oracle about how best to cure their ills.

8. As noted earlier, Sade is referring to himself, and specifically to the Marseilles affair that was the source of so many of his later woes.

9. A lawgiver of Sparta, probably ninth century B.C.

10. On the southern tip of the Peloponnesian Peninsula.

11. Averroës (1126–1198). An Arab philosopher and doctor, best known for his commentaries on Aristotle. What perhaps endeared him to Sade was that, like himself, this Arab doctor was a social outcast, his views on pantheism having been roundly condemned by the learned doctors of the Sorbonne. (See "The Teacher Philosopher.")

12. Again, Sade is portraying himself as the victim. During the month of August 1778, a band of law enforcement officers, in the service of and paid by Sade's mother-in-law, invaded his castle at La

Coste in southern France, and arrested the marquis, under much the same circumstances he describes here.

13. Sade's pun eludes translation. While the tribunal's benches were adorned with the fleur-de-lis, the coat of arms of the French royal family, the author is doubtless referring to the barbaric practice of branding criminals with fleurs-de-lis.

14. Again, Sade is referring to himself and the Marseilles episode.

15. Sade's memory fails him by a year. He is doubtless referring to what has become known as the Arceuil affair, which took place on April 3, 1768. Sade accosted a certain Rose Keller that morning on the Place de Victoires and took her to his rented cottage in the Paris suburb of Arceuil. There, he submitted her to "the English vice"; escaping from Sade's cottage, she lodged a complaint against him, and a short time later Sade was arrested and incarcerated in the Pierre-Encize prison near Lyons.

16. The Law of Talion, which dates back to early Hebrew and Greek history—and later to Roman—demands retribution in kind. More commonly, we know it as "an eye for an eye, a tooth for a tooth." See earlier reference to *lex talionis* on page 35.

17. Paphos, on the island of Cyprus, was famous for its temple to Venus. In eighteenth-century parlance "temples of Venus" referred to brothels.

18. A name meaning pure, chaste. Saint Agnes was a Christian martyr of the fourth century, a virgin who, having refused several suitors because of her "marriage" to Christ, was sent to a brothel as punishment. The first young man who touched her was struck blind, but after she prayed for him he regained his sight. She was executed shortly thereafter.

19. This prescient sentence was written, as noted, just two years before the French Revolution.

20. Mérindol is a town near Apt in the region of Provence where, in 1545, Protestants were massacred in great numbers.

21. In the eighteenth century, the French king could issue, at his pleasure so to speak, a *lettre de cachet*—literally a document bearing

the king's seal—which had the virtue of overriding any court's decision or sentence, that is, removing an accused from the normal judicial process. The other side of that royal coin was that, under a *lettre de cachet*, a person could be imprisoned, without appeal, for as long as the king liked. Sade spent more than twelve years in the royal dungeons under such a *lettre de cachet*.

EMILIE DE TOURVILLE OR FRATERNAL CRUELTY

1. Sade himself, as his father before him, bore the title of lieutenant-general, which was more hereditary and honorable than its bellicose name implies. It was largely an honorary title, but carried with it an income that could be substantial.

2. A street that no longer exists, though it did in Sade's time. In the mid-nineteenth century it was incorporated into the rue Saint-Martin in Paris's third arrondissement. No doubt Sade would be tickled by the fact that today it is a playground for prostitutes.

3. There are no hard figures relative to the number of prostitutes—not to mention hardworking women so poor they needed to supplement their income—plying their trade in eighteenth-century Paris. Here Sade, through the intermediary of Madame Berceil, is suggesting that many women of quality were also selling their favors. Be that as it may, there was at the time a substantial vice squad within the Paris police monitoring the brothels. In fact, Sade's name figures prominently in its reports.

4. Coucy-le-Château, a town bordering the Saint-Germain forest. Noyan is a town on the Compiègne-San-Quentin road.

5. In his novels as in his letters, Sade often rails against those who take justice into their own hands and punish those they fear or dislike. In the eighteenth century, any well-placed or aristocratic family (they were not always one and the same) could petition the king to issue the aforementioned *lettre de cachet*. Armed with such a document, a family could have a person—usually another family member one wanted to get rid of—incarcerated in perpetuity. Here, through the character of the Count de Luxeuil, Sade is comparing the hate-

ful Tourville brothers to his mother-in-law, la présidente de Montreuil, who because of misdeeds, real and presumed, did indeed petition the king to have the marquis arrested and was instrumental in keeping him locked up until the Revolution, when the *lettre de cachet* was abolished and Sade released. (See note 20 for "The Mystified Magistrate.")

6. The song Sade cites is not from the region in which his tale is set but, understandably, from his native Provence.

7. This is one of the rare times Sade speaks well of a member of the judiciary, whose corruption he views as one of the basic reasons he is behind bars. One will note that Judge Tourville has quit the bench because, being intelligent, gentle, and of excellent character, he could not stand the stench of the place.

8. The private individual Sade clearly has in mind here is his hated mother-in-law, Madame de Montreuil, who, in Sade's view, had him punished for his "crimes."

AUGUSTINE DE VILLEBRANCHE
OR LOVE'S STRATEGY

1. Sappho (circa 612 B.C.) is one of the most famous lyric poets of all time. Although she was married and had a daughter, and cast herself into the sea to commit suicide over the unrequited love of the uncommonly handsome young man Phoas, her name is generally associated with lesbianism, from the name of the island where she lived most of her life, Lesbos. Many of her poems are indeed addressed to women, and she was the leader of a group of girls devoted to music and poetry.

2. Two famous jurists of the fourteenth and sixteenth centuries, respectively: the Italian Bartolo (1313–1357) and the Frenchman Jacques Cujas (1520–1590; see note 2 for "The Mystified Magistrate"). Louis IX (1214–1270) was instrumental during his long reign in reforming the French legal system, creating a judiciary commission that laid the foundation for a future parliament.

3. In Greek mythology, the Graces were three goddesses, the daughters of Zeus, who enhanced the pleasures of life: Aglaia (brilliance), Euphrosyne (joy), and Thalia (bloom).

4. See note 16 for "The Mystified Magistrate."

5. Antinoüs was a young man of whom the Emperor Hadrian was uncommonly fond. Psyche, in Greek mythology, was a maiden of uncommon beauty with whom Cupid fell madly in love (not Adonis, as Sade states). She is a symbol of immortality.

THE PROPERLY PUNISHED PIMP

1. Upon the death of Louis XIV in 1715, his successor Louis XV was only five years old. Accordingly, Philippe d'Orleans was appointed regent until the young king was of age. If the golden age of the Sun King had been marked by an almost unprecedented state of immorality within the court and throughout the realm, the regent did nothing to improve matters. If anything, he made them worse (that remark is meant historically, not as a moral judgment), setting an example for Louis XV who, if anything, improved on Louis XIV's practices.

2. There is no rue des Déjeuners (literally, Breakfast Street) in Paris, nor to my knowledge has there ever been one. Sade probably means the rue des Jeûneurs, near the Paris Bourse, the stock exchange. In the author's day it was on the outskirts of town, a place where Parisians gathered to play various outdoor games such as *boules*. Originally known as the rue des Jeux-neufs (literally, New Games Street) its name was subsequently corrupted to its present spelling. Today the street, which is in the second arrondissement, runs between the rue des Victoires and rue Poissonnière.

3. In "The Mystified Magistrate," La Brie is also the name given to Count d'Elbène when he is passing as a valet. In life, Sade enjoyed giving nicknames or false names to his own valets. Clearly this is a favorite name of Sade's.

4. Sade is in all probability referring to Philippe de Bourbon, who died in 1727 and held the distinguished title of Grand Prieur of

France, though he might have been targeting his older brother, Louis-Joseph de Bourbon. Since, despite his impressive apostolic title, Philippe was a well-known libertine, chances are it was the younger Bourbon Sade was implicating here.

THE TEACHER PHILOSOPHER

1. A common exclamation, long outdated, a corruption of, or euphemism for, *ventredieu*, literally "God's belly."

AN EYE FOR AN EYE

1. Sade's irony is showing. The reference is to the Count de Tressan, an older contemporary of Sade, who was largely responsible in the eighteenth century for the revival of interest in medieval literature, which Sade despised, as evidenced in his introduction to his own *The Crimes of Love*, published in 1800, in which he summarily dismisses medieval romances as "long and boring."

2. Again, the reference is ironic, for this town in northeastern France located on the Somme River is famous as the scene of a bloody battle that took place there in 1557, but, at least up until Sade's day, and to the best of my knowledge since, has never given the world any writer of note.

3. As a playwright, Sade was acutely aware of the trends in contemporary theater. The reference here is obscure, but what he seems to be suggesting is that, given the technical advances in graphics and the increased appetite of the public for prints and artistic reproductions in the late eighteenth century, producers would opt for a play whose subject could be easily depicted graphically in the press and elsewhere rather than on the merits of the play itself. Today, we would think of that as merchandising. Because Sade, however in advance of his time he was in many things, was a good (or actually, bad) old-fashioned playwright, he had to be irked by what he considered

unfair criteria for getting a play put on in Paris. Once he was set free in 1790, he spent a great deal of time trying to have his own plays produced, to little avail.

4. An unlikely number of years, since even considering the tendency of the time to marry young, that unparalleled period of fidelity had to put the good lady well over a hundred. Several times in his collection of stories, Sade's numbers are inconsistent or contradictory, doubtless a result of not always having the opportunity to correct his initial drafts.

5. The same Lucrece who served as the subject for Shakespeare's *The Rape of Lucrece*. Having been brutally raped, the lady committed suicide, choosing death to dishonor and, in life as well as in Shakespeare, symbolizing the supreme act of purity and chastity.

THE WINDBAGS OF PROVENCE

1. In case everyone doesn't know, there actually was during the long reign of Louis XIV an ambassador to France from Persia, a gentleman named Mahemet Riza Bey, who many members of the French court and intellectuals of the day, including Saint Simon, thought was a fraud. In fact, he was authentic.

2. Throughout his literary work, and in his voluminous letters, Sade has a fixation on the question of magistrates taking the side of prostitutes whenever disputes between them and their clients are brought to court. Sade's view—and indeed the prevailing opinion of the time—was that if a man paid for a lady's favors, the bargain struck obviated any legal recourse on the part of the one who had accepted the money. Despite this, Sade was arrested, tried, and sent to prison on at least three occasions on the basis of complaints lodged against him by these "clients."

3. François I (1494–1547), king of France from 1515 to 1547, was an accomplished ruler in both foreign and domestic matters, and is credited with laying the first firm foundations of the absolute monarchy of the *ancien régime*. Despite all his accomplishments, he is also sadly remembered—and it is this that Sade refers to here—for his

merciless persecution and massacre of the Protestants in southern France.

4. From Areopagus, the Hill of Ares where in antiquity the Athens tribunal sat in judgment. As he often does, Sade uses classical references in his stories and novels, both to display his erudition—which was considerable—and doubtless to impress any would-be censors.

5. Two towns in the Vaucluse region of southern France not far from Sade's château at La Coste. Again, Sade is reminding his readers of the bloody Protestant persecutions of the sixteenth century, at the instigation of François I. The tie-in here with the eighteenth-century judges of Aix is that the massacre of Protestants two centuries earlier occurred under the leadership of a High Court justice of Aix, one Meynier d'Oppède.

ROOM FOR TWO

1. *Venus of Callipygus,* from the two Greek words *kallos*—beauty—plus *pygi*—buttocks. A work in the Farnese collection in Naples, which Sade visited the year before his Vincennes imprisonment, this statue was one of the most beautiful portrayals of the goddess of beauty and love ever made. The statue is cited by Sade dozens of times in his works, since that part of the female—or indeed human—anatomy held a special interest for him.

THE HUSBAND WHO TURNED PRIEST: A TALE OF PROVENCE

1. Two towns in the Vaucluse region of France, the former a hill town in the Luberan mountains only about three or four miles from Sade's château at La Coste. Apt, about ten miles away to the east, was the county seat of the region, where dwelt the marquis's lawyer, a man named Gaufridy, to whom Sade entrusted his business affairs for several decades. The region described is one Sade knows intimately.

2. The convent of Saint-Hilaire still stands today, a mile or two from Menerbe (which two centuries after this tale was penned became the site of Peter Mayle's *A Year in Provence*) on the road to La Coste. In Sade's time it was indeed a Carmelite monastery (today it is privately owned), but there is no indication in any historical records I could find that any "Father Gabriel" ever dwelt within its not-so-hallowed walls, or that the moral qualities (or lack thereof) of its inhabitants were as Sade described.

3. The main castle of the area was Sade's own, at La Coste.

4. According to tradition, the Carmelite order traces its roots back to the prophet Elijah.

5. A local wine of the Vaucluse region, with which in all probability Sade had direct experience. One of today's best Chateauneuf du Pape wines is from Château la Nerthe, which may well be a descendent of Father Gabriel's vintage.

6. Sade may be referring here to his own dear wife, Renée-Pélagie de Montreuil de Sade, who spent a great deal of her life trying to explain away or atone for her husband's misdeeds. At the time these stories were written, Sade had been in prison for seven years, and in the Bastille for three, and during the later years of his incarceration, Madame de Sade lived in the Paris convent of Saint Aure, where she increasingly came under the influence of the Church and her father confessor, who urged her to work not only to save her own soul but that of her husband. She may well have accomplished the former, certainly not the latter.

7. Until 1789, Sade himself was lord of the manor of La Coste and the surrounding area. In pre-revolutionary times, hunting on the land owned by the local noble—in other words, poaching—was subject to the severest penalties under the law. Further, only nobles were allowed to bear arms, so the very fact that Rodin and Father Gabriel were out shooting game was a crime in itself.

8. As noted, there are sometimes contradictions in numbers and figures in some of Sade's stories, essentially because, as noted earlier, only the penultimate version of these tales came down to us, the so-called "Yellow Notebook," which did not contain the author's final corrections. Earlier, Madame Rodin was twenty-eight. I'm sure she

still was, on the day her husband said mass, and Sade's suddenly making her six years younger is a slip of his usually careful pen.

THIEVES AND SWINDLERS

1. Carnival time in France in Sade's day was the last week before Lent.

2. The rue Quincampoix, which still exists today, runs between the rue aux Ours and the rue des Lombards in what today are Paris's third and fourth arrondissements. For four centuries before Sade's time, it had been the site of the Drapers Guild, one of Paris's richest. Rosette's uncle Mathieu was not the only wealthy money-lender to live there. In "The Misfortunes of Virtue" and *Justine*, the "money-lender" (in "Misfortunes") and the "famous Parisian usurer" (in *Justine*), both odious misers (who are one and the same), live on the rue Quincampoix.

3. On the Normandy-Paris route, Pontoise was a coach stop about twenty miles from central Paris. In the eighteenth century it was the next-to-last stop before reaching the city center.

4. On the outskirts of Paris. This was the last coach stop prior to reaching the city center. Clearly the coachman in whose care Rosette had been placed by her father failed miserably in his task.

5. Sade here is remembering, fondly or not, a church with which he is familiar. It was there, on May 17, 1763, that he and Renée-Pélagie de Montreuil were married.

THE GASCON WIT

1. A region of southwestern France bounded on its western side by the Bay of Biscay. The thick Gascon accent is the butt of frequent jokes on the part of other French regions, as is the region's tendencies to embellish hard facts on the one hand and wiggle out of deals

on the other. Indeed, *faire le Gascon* means "to beg or boast"; and *un offre de Gascon*—a Gascon offer—means a hollow offer.

2. Jean-Baptiste Colbert (1619–1683). Under Louis XIV, the indefatigable minister with several portfolios; he was successively superintendent of building under the Sun King, controller of finance, and secretary of state. He was also a staunch supporter of French arts and letters, and for the last twenty years of his life was a member of the French Academy. The very notion that an unknown and unannounced officer could barge into Colbert's Versailles quarters brings Sade reasonably close to the Theater of the Absurd.

3. A variant of *cadédiou*, a mild Gascon swearword.